Green Mountain Academy

GREEN MOUNTAIN ACADEMY

Frances Greenslade

tundra

Tundra Books, an imprint of Tundra Book Group,
a division of Penguin Random House of Canada Limited

Library and Archives Canada Cataloguing in Publication

Title: Green Mountain Academy / Frances Greenslade.
Names: Greenslade, Frances, 1961– author.
Identifiers: Canadiana (print) 20210351802 | Canadiana (ebook)
20210351837 | ISBN 9780735267848 (hardcover) |
ISBN 9780735267855 (EPUB)
Subjects: LCGFT: Novels.
Classification: LCC PS8613 R438 G74 2022 | DDC jC813/.6—dc23

Published simultaneously in the United States of America by
Tundra Books of Northern New York, an imprint of Tundra Book Group,
a division of Penguin Random House of Canada Limited

Library of Congress Control Number: 2021949258

Edited by Lynne Missen
Jacket designed by John Martz
The text was set in Perpetua

Printed in the United States of America

www.penguinrandomhouse.ca

1st Printing

For Neil and Chase Greenslade,
who understand courage.

CHAPTER ONE

Pitch dark, the kind of dark that's so dark, colors swirl, pulsing before my eyes. I could be at the edge of a bottomless pit, for all I could see. A dank smell of old, old mud rose up. Sounds rolled like thunder in my ears, then the roar of my own blood beating stopped them altogether and the world dropped away. I was nowhere, anywhere, held up by emptiness. Was I falling or floating? The sting of my fall vibrated through my legs. I reeled forward, catching my hands in midair, but I was already on the ground. Under my knees, loose shale crunched.

My knees were probably bleeding. They hurt. But what hurt worse was that I didn't make it. Again.

I took a deep breath. Slowly, my eyes adjusted to the blank darkness of the cave. A patch of something paler took shape, like a cloud forming. I crawled toward it. Then a crack of light opened above my head and a hand appeared, reaching down.

"Francie! Are you all right?"

Danny's face appeared in the daylight and she grinned at me. I could see my headlamp where it rolled after I fell.

"I'm okay. But I didn't make it. Obviously."

"Okay, I'm lowering the rope."

A snake of rope pierced the light, twisted down toward me.

"Have you got it?"

I picked up my headlamp and slung it around my neck. Then I grabbed hold of the rope. "I've got it."

"I'm ready!" Danny shouted.

"Danny?" My voice sounded far away in the echoing cave.

"I've got you."

"No. I want to try again."

"It's getting late. We've got to be back before supper."

"I know. Just one more try."

"Aren't you tired? You probably shouldn't try when you're tired."

"I almost had it. Once I'm past that ledge, I'm home free. And I was so close."

"Okay. But remember, the higher you go, the more dangerous it is if you fall."

"Danny?"

"What?"

"Are you going to tell me to be careful?"

She laughed. "I was thinking of it, actually."

Danny hated it when I, or anybody, told her to be careful. She'd answer in her driest voice, "Actually, my plan was to be as reckless as possible and risk my own life and the lives of others."

The rockface I was trying to climb was a few feet away from where Danny was. Our rope wasn't long enough to tie to the only sturdy tree nearby and still reach the hole where I'd climb out—if I made it. So I was on my own. Another fall would really hurt. But I was determined not to fall again. My climbing skills

2

were getting better; I just needed to find a way around the bulge of rock where I hadn't been able to find any handholds. Last time, I'd made a lunge for one and missed. That's how I ended up in the mud.

I shook out the jitters in my arms and legs and took a deep breath.

"It's doable, Francie," Danny called.

That was Danny in a nutshell. Most things were "doable" to her. It was one of the things I liked about her. I turned on my headlamp, then looked up at the rockface. It shone in the light, little trails of water snaking down and turning the black rock slick in places. It could be done, I was sure of it. I stepped onto the rockface, jamming the toe of my runners into a foothold. Then I had an idea.

I jumped back down and took off my runners and socks, shoved them in my jacket pockets. Then I tried again. My bare toes found the footholds in the cool damp rock. It was easier to feel them this way. My hands sought the familiar fingerholds, clung to them, and I swung myself up, covering the first part of the climb in just a couple of minutes. But I was tired.

I rested my cheek flat against the wet rock and let the jitters calm. My feet were losing feeling. Maybe bare feet hadn't been such a great idea. After all, it was November and colder in these mountains than down in the valley.

"Don't rest too long, Francie," Danny called. "You'll lose your strength."

She was right. It was now or never. If I held on much longer, my legs and arms would turn to jelly and I might not have the strength to climb back down if I didn't make it. And

I didn't want to fall again. With another burst of effort, I reached up and found an edge for the fingers of my right hand. If I could only get my leg up somewhere. But I tried a few spots and my toe slipped off each time. I tried to find a hold for my left hand. My fingers slid over cold stone. I stopped again, my hands burning and my muscles quivering. I could see the sky now, a washed-out gray, low cloud like fog skimming across it.

There was that small outcropping. But it was just out of reach, no matter how much I stretched myself. Lunging for it was how I'd fallen before.

"Francie?"

"Yeah."

"It's snowing."

"Okay."

"I think we should go."

I ran my hand over the rockface once more, searching for somewhere to move. But there was nothing.

"Okay. I'm climbing down."

"I'll meet you at the other hole. Hey! Be careful!"

I smiled, lowering myself on stiff fingers and toes that had lost all feeling. Then I crawled along the ground to the other opening. My hands shook as I pulled my socks over my ice-cold feet, then slipped on my runners. It was hard to tie my shoe-laces. My heart was still pattering like a woodpecker.

There was no need to climb this rockface. I'd discovered it when I'd deliberately climbed through the tunnel of rock, squirming on my belly in places, exploring, to see how far I could get and if there was a way out. What made me want to do it? Danny understood. Most of the time, she didn't even try to talk me out of it.

After Ms. Fineday, who had been my teacher before—and me—no one else I knew loved being out in the woods as much as Danny. Danny's great-uncle Charlie was a guide in their family's traditional territory in northern British Columbia. He took people hunting and fishing and canoeing and hiking into deep wilderness, where grizzlies and wolves and eagles lived, and where making mistakes could cost you your life. Danny had been sure he'd hire her to work for him this past summer. She'd spent the summer before with him, learning to read a river, to understand riffles and eddies and runs, and she'd learned paddle strokes and how not to blow a stalk when following an animal in the woods. But instead he took on her cousin Rudy, a boy, she told me, who'd rather find his way through video games than the actual forest.

"I can't believe he did that," Danny had said when she told me. "He said it was because I'm only thirteen and I need more practical experience. Next summer's going to be different."

I took hold of the dangling rope and with the last of my strength twisted my way up.

Danny gripped my arm around hers and hoisted me out onto the rock.

"Look at the sky," she said. "We're in for some serious snow. It's going to get slippery in here very soon."

Danny and I had made a secret trail down to this area we'd discovered about half an hour from our school, Green Mountain Academy. We called it the Sasquatch Caves. They weren't proper caves; a field of huge boulders piled on top of each other formed a labyrinth of holes and passages, some of them big enough to be called caves. Danny said this was the kind of hangout Sasquatches liked.

It was treacherous walking through there even when it was dry. We had to watch we didn't slip or take a wrong step into a crack that had no bottom. Then it was a scramble over the boulders to the base of a wall of rock to get back on the path we'd made. Once we climbed the wall, the bench of pine-forested land opened up and we would follow the winding track we called Secret Trail back to Fire Tower Trail, which led to the school.

Fire Tower Trail was the main trail around Green Mountain Academy. You could pick it up from the back yard, behind the clothesline and the compost area, and it led first to the old fire tower, a lookout about half a mile from the school. Then it made a circle route through the woods, across a big meadow, with a side trail down to Smoky Creek, then through more pine forest and back to the school.

No one knew about the path Danny and I had made to the caves except Danny and me and Ming Yue, an older girl we'd told because she's a climber and we wanted advice. We'd found the caves late in September when we were exploring the woods. According to the school rules, we were supposed to stay within the bounds of Fire Tower Trail, but Danny and I figured that adventure meant sometimes going out of bounds.

The sign at the end of the driveway up to our school says *Green Mountain Academy: Adventure School for Girls.* How I ended up there is a long story and one I don't like to think about if I can help it.

We pulled up the rope where we'd anchored it and I untied it, then put it in a garbage bag at the base of the tree. Then we picked our way across the boulders that were growing more slippery as the snow fell. In a couple places, we squatted and used our hands to move along.

It was an easy climb up the rockface, with jutting rocks that were almost like stairs. As Danny and I hurried along the path through the pine forest, things began to disappear. First, the sky melted away in the blur of fast-falling snow, then the trees ahead became a thickening curtain of white, and then our path petered out and one opening in the trees looked like every other one—snow-covered, windswept.

Danny, who was ahead, shouted something. The wind picked up her voice and carried it up and away through the trees. I caught up to her and grabbed her arm.

"Are you sure you're going the right way?" I had to shout over the rising wind.

She stopped. "I lost the path a while back, but I'm pretty sure."

"I didn't bring my compass, did you?"

"No. I mean, we've come this way twenty times at least. If we keep heading this way, we should run into Fire Tower Trail. This seems right, doesn't it?"

I knew that just because a direction feels right doesn't mean it is right. Dad had walked into the Oregon wilderness in what seemed like the right direction. I still remember watching him in his yellow rain jacket, his pack hoisted on his back, as he disappeared into the rain. That was the last time I ever saw him.

Danny had set off again.

"Wait, Danny," I called.

She stopped. "We're going to be late for dinner."

"If we get lost, we'll be even later. Just stop for a minute. Let's be sure about where we are."

She huffed a little impatiently.

I'd known Danny now for less than three months, but I knew she didn't like to sit still. She always had a new idea about places to hike, or rocks to climb, or forts to build. After lights out in the room we shared, she worked out her ideas out loud. Sometimes I fell asleep to the sound of her thoughtful voice, low and sleepy, as she weighed possibilities for new adventures.

I was the one who made sure we had the right equipment—ropes, flashlights, compass, water, food and extra jackets. I checked the weather forecast on the radio and then double-checked with the sky, since the forecast only really applied to town, and up here we had our own little weather system. This time, I'd only told Ming where we were going. Lill and Lucy, the owners of the school, were away, and I knew that Ms. Benito, who was filling in, would want us to stay close to the school. She was a good cook and all the girls liked her, but she had no sense of adventure.

Danny and I sat on a rock now and caught our breath. Wind drove the snow sideways, peppering our faces. Up higher, it roared through the treetops, stirring them crazily. The thick-falling snow had blotted out what was left of the day. Dusk descended quickly, and with it, the familiar dread. My heartbeat did little skips, like a bicycle chain catching in the gears. Ever since the days and nights I spent alone in the middle of the Oregon wilderness, I'd had to fight this feeling: that when dusk came on it wasn't only the day that was over—everything was over.

"Hey," said Danny. "You okay?"

"Just thinking."

"It's beautiful, though, right? I love the smell of snow, don't you?"

I looked at Danny's hands on her blue-jeaned knees. Her warm eyes studied me. Danny told me once that walking in the woods made the world disappear. I only realized at this moment that I'd never questioned why anyone would want the world to disappear. I just knew.

"It's going to be a crazy storm tonight," she said now. "It'll be fun."

"Only you would say that." I smiled.

"Or you," she said.

"Do you recognize anything?"

She looked around, then stood and made a circle, scanning the woods. "I think maybe . . . Look! Isn't that the bent pine tree we usually pass?"

"I think you're right."

"Come on!" She grabbed my hand and we scrambled over fallen logs to the tree.

It was our tree, a ponderosa pine that had a large branch bent like a pointing arm in the direction of the caves.

"And, look, here's our path," said Danny. "We *were* a little off track."

Just then a strange buzzing noise filled the air overhead, like a giant swarm of bees. It grew louder and then faded just as quickly.

"What was that?" I said, straining to hear it in the wind.

"It sounded like a plane."

"Pretty low for a plane," I said.

"Come on. Let's hurry," said Danny.

It was easier walking now that we knew where we were. We leaned into the rising wind that seemed about to sweep us off the trail. I followed Danny, happy to let her lead the way. After about twenty minutes, the bulky shape of the fire tower loomed out of the flurry of driving snow.

"We're almost back. There's the school."

We crested the hill behind the school and saw the clothesline, frozen sheets still pinned to the line and twisting into bunches in the wind.

"Let's grab these sheets!" Danny shouted as she ran ahead.

As we fought to free the sheets from the tangle of clothespins, Ming bounded out the back door, dressed only in a flannel shirt, jeans and runners.

"What took you guys? I thought I was going to have to cover for you at dinner. Everything's on the table already."

Danny dumped a pile of snowy sheets in Ming's arms. "Things took a little longer than planned."

Ming's full name was Ming Yue, she'd told us on the first day, which meant "bright moon." I thought that was the nicest name I'd ever heard. "It's not bad," Ming had agreed. "But I've been called Ming since kindergarten."

At fifteen, Ming was older than us, but she was our best friend at the school—apart from each other. She loved to climb and had all the right gear—proper climbing shoes, a harness and rope, a helmet, and a whole bunch of orange and green and black carabiners. She spent her summers climbing at Skaha Bluffs and could climb grades of 5.10, which, apparently, was pretty hard. But she wouldn't lend us any gear. Not that we'd asked, but when she found out we were climbing in the caves, she'd told us, "I'm not lending you gear because, until you learn to use it properly, it's probably more dangerous than no gear at all."

She did come out to the caves now and then to give us tips. Like how to hang from your arms, keeping them straight, instead of trying to cling to the rock using the strength of your biceps. And to keep most of your weight on your legs, not your arms. It takes technique and flexibility, not just arm strength. That's why girls could be such good climbers, she said. Even small girls like me.

"Ms. Benito made spaghetti," Ming said now. "Hurry up! It's freezing out here."

In the vestibule, we brushed the snow from our clothes and hair and put our shoes on the rack to dry. It was good to be inside with the heat blowing from the vents. A heavenly rich smell of garlic and onions and spices wafted from the kitchen.

Ms. Benito had her back to us as she wiped the stove. She turned when we came in.

"Oh, thank goodness. I was really starting to worry. And look, you brought the sheets in. Aren't you good girls?"

Danny smiled at me.

"Supper's on the table. I made my famous spaghetti sauce. You must be starving."

"I am," I said, passing my armload of sheets to Ms. Benito's outstretched arms.

"Me too," said Danny.

"Well, I'm glad you're back," Ms. Benito said again. "The sisters would never forgive me if I lost two of you the first night they're away."

CHAPTER TWO

"The sisters" were Lucy and Lill, the school founders and teachers. Everyone called them the sisters when they weren't around, because it was easier. But we were allowed to call them by their first names when we were with them, since calling them both Ms. Larsen would have been too confusing.

The day Aunt Sissy and Ms. Fineday drove me out to meet them, Aunt Sissy had borrowed Grandpa's SUV because she'd been told the road was rough for the last thirty kilometers or so. It was rough, but it was also beautiful. Rolling hills dotted with sage became soft, grassy meadows—yellow at that time of year—then big fluttering cottonwoods around a small lake, then a creek, almost dry, then more trees crowding the road. The landscape became a little wilder, the woods a little thicker. The farther we went, the more Aunt Sissy talked.

"Now, you can change your mind about this, Francie. For any reason."

"Okay."

A few minutes later: "If there's the slightest thing that gives you doubts, you tell me. Okay?"

"Uh-huh." I nodded.

"And I mean anything."

"Yup."

"If one of them even looks at you funny, that's all I need to pull the plug."

"I know."

Ms. Fineday turned around in the front seat and smiled at me. I wasn't worried, and I think she knew that. She knew that the wilder the landscape, the more I liked it. Lonely places didn't scare me—not anymore. They seemed like old friends. I got a shiver when the swaying trees reminded me of the cave on the creek bank in Oregon where I had spent a night protected from a wild windstorm, but it wasn't a shiver of fear now.

Ms. Fineday had been my teacher at my school in Penticton. I didn't know anyone who knew as much about the outdoors as she did. The sisters were her friends, and it was Ms. Fineday who'd first told me about the school. That was in the summer. After everything had happened. After I was home safely to a place that didn't feel like home at all anymore.

"Staying with Grandpa is out of the question," Aunt Sissy continued, as if thinking out loud. "But moving to the city with me is still an option. I just thought you might like this better."

"I know. It's okay, Aunt Sissy. I want to go to the school," I said.

"Now what did I say about not deciding until you actually saw it? You can't just go with a gut feeling. Let's wait for the evidence."

Aunt Sissy is a lawyer, and she liked to remind me to look for evidence before I made my decisions. But I'd seen pictures.

Also, Ms. Fineday had taught some special outdoors classes at the school, so I was pretty sure already.

It's amazing the things you learn when adults suddenly think you're old enough. *After everything happened*—which was the way Aunt Sissy and I both referred to that time—and I had to stay with Grandpa, Aunt Sissy told me that he had a "drinking problem." That explained why he disappeared into his room every night after supper. Come to think of it, it explained a few things: why I heard him stumbling around the house after I went to bed; why, before everything happened, we used to get calls at odd hours of the night from Grandpa's neighbors and Dad would get dressed and go out. When I asked where he'd gone, he'd always say the same thing: Grandpa was upset.

"What is he always upset about?" I once asked Aunt Sissy.

"That was a euphemism," she told me.

"What's a euphemism?"

"Not calling a spade a spade. If there's one thing I have no patience with, it's that."

I didn't like to hear her say that, because I thought it meant she had no patience with Dad.

As if reading my mind, she said, "I'm not criticizing your dad. What else could he say to a little girl?"

"But what was Grandpa upset about?"

"Well, sweetheart, I've asked myself that my whole life. And I discovered it's no use asking."

After a minute or two of silence, I realized she had no more to say about that.

"Well, since Grandpa is Mom's and your father," I said, "why did Dad go to him when he was upset?"

"*Because* he's your mom's dad. Your mom just can't stand to be around him when he's into the sauce. He'd never hurt anyone—I wouldn't let you stay with him a minute if there was any chance of that."

"I know."

"Grandma couldn't stand it either. That's why she went to live at the cabin at Gem Lake. She said she wanted to live out her last days in peace and quiet and he could stay in the city and weather his storms the way he'd always done. She'd given up hoping he'd turn over a new leaf."

I only partly understood what all of that meant, and I thought that for someone who had no patience with euphemisms, Aunt Sissy used a lot of them.

In those first days after Aunt Sissy brought me home from Oregon without Mom and Dad, Grandpa and Aunt Sissy sat at the kitchen table in Grandpa's house, the house where Aunt Sissy and Mom grew up. The shadows of leaves in sunlight danced on the window and they drank cups and cups of tea and tried to decide what to do with me. The only thing I heard Grandpa say about it was, "She'll decide when she's ready." Aunt Sissy nodded, more quiet than I'd ever seen her. Sometimes I saw one or the other of them with tears running down their faces.

Maybe it's selfish of me, but I was glad.

Living with Grandpa that summer, after everything had happened, was about the most depressing thing I could have done. His routines became like a dull ringing in my ears. I couldn't escape the sad sameness of it. Every morning he took a packet of instant oatmeal from a box, ran some water over it and stuck it in the microwave. He made a mug of tea from the same teabag he'd used for his supper tea the night before, then he sat out on the step and smoked a cigarette.

When he came back inside, I braced myself for his inevitable comment about me reading too much.

"You'll spoil your eyes, Francie."

"Don't you think it's time you got some fresh air?"

"How many books can one person read?"

And, "Aren't those books for babies?"

It was true I was reading books that Mom used to read to me when my twin sister Phoebe and I were little. I'd brought a box of them from our house. My favorite was *Can't You Sleep, Little Bear?*

Because I couldn't sleep. Or not much. Or not at night when I was supposed to. After supper, when we'd finished washing our two plates, two glasses, two knives and two forks, Grandpa would say good night and take his chipped Tim Hortons mug with him into his room. I would pull some books from the box I'd brought from our house and read on my bed. Every hour or so I heard him come out of his room and go into the kitchen, and with each trip he got noisier. First a few cupboards slamming, water running for a long time; then later, chairs falling over, his grumbling as he bumped into things; and in the middle of the night things falling to the floor, sometimes the crash of breaking glass.

I stayed put in my room, the little guest room under the stairs with the slanted ceiling, which, when the moonlight lit up the walls, I imagined was a mountainside. In the morning, it was as if nothing had happened, and when I saw Grandpa at the table drinking his watered-down tea from his chipped mug, I wondered if I'd dreamt it. Then I'd sleep mid-morning, about two hours after I got up, or in the afternoon while Grandpa dozed with his mouth open in the worn recliner in front of the TV droning on the nature channel.

I didn't eat much either. I suppose it didn't help that everything Grandpa ate came from a can or a box: Spam, fish sticks, frozen Salisbury steaks, canned beans or corn.

"I'm not much of a cook," he said one night when he put a plate of canned peas and a slice of Spam down in front of me. "You're welcome to try yourself if you think you can do better."

I wasn't much of a cook either, but I was pretty sure it wouldn't take much to do better. But I wasn't going to hurt his feelings by trying. And anyway, I had no appetite.

He took me on drives to sit and watch the birds at Vaseux Lake. We stopped at Okanagan Falls and had ice cream. I didn't want to tell Grandpa that I'd never really liked ice cream; it was my twin sister, Phoebe, who'd liked ice cream. She was the one he used to take to Tickleberry's, the famous ice cream stand, not me, and it was Phoebe who liked Tiger Tiger ice cream, not me. But he was trying so hard.

He tried to get me to invite my friends over.

I called Carly and we walked over to the school playground and hung off the monkey bars the way we used to after school. It felt like such a long time ago. She talked about things and I nodded but when I went to speak, there was nothing there. I worried that I might never speak again. I couldn't see the point in it.

Grandpa went to our house again, Mom's and Dad's and my house, and brought back my bike from the shed. He leaned it by the back step and hosed the cobwebs off it. Then he oiled the chain and tightened up my brakes. Now, mornings, he had a new thing to nag me about.

"Good day for a ride," he'd say, coming in after his cigarette.

Or, "We need milk. You can pop down to the store on your bike."

People phoned or came to the door and Grandpa nodded, saying, "Uh-huh, uh-huh" and "Well, that's something to think about."

If your parents ever disappear into the wilderness while you're on a family vacation, you'll find that an awful lot of people will have strong opinions about what should be done with you. Many of those people won't even know you, but they'll take your aunt and your grandpa aside and they'll lower their voices a little and they'll say things like, "I'm sure she'll want things to stay as normal as possible." And by that they'll mean you should stay in your old neighborhood and go to your old school and take up all your old activities. They'll recommend routine, to try to make things "normal."

But the thing that none of those people will understand is that nothing is normal anymore. Your old house will look strange and sad and empty, with windows like lonely eyes watching for its people to return; the path up the creek where you rode your bike will feel like another country; and even your bike will feel awkward and unsteady and you'll barely remember how you used to ride it so fast and smooth, like it was another part of your body. They won't understand that trying to be normal in your old life that's exploded is the worst feeling in the world.

CHAPTER THREE

I met Danny on the first of September, my first official day at the school. It was a perfect day, everything crisp and bright in the golden sunlight, a clear turquoise-blue sky and no wind. Some of the trees up Green Mountain had begun to turn, just here and there, a super yellow-green. Insects and birds sang from the woods as Lill helped me carry my bags to my room.

"This is Danielle, your roommate," Lill said as we entered the room. A girl with short dark hair wearing faded jeans and a soft red T-shirt had her back to us as she reached to put a suit-case on the top shelf of the closet.

She turned. Her bright eyes studied me. "Don't call me Danielle. I'm Danny." She thrust her hand at me; it took me a few seconds to realize I was supposed to shake it. I don't know if I'd ever shaken someone's hand before, and definitely never someone's my own age.

"Sorry, Danny," said Lill. "How could I forget that? I was named Lillian after my grandmother, but I've been Lill since I was a baby. Everyone could see I wasn't a Lillian."

"What's your name?" said Danny, her voice more a command than a question.

"Francie," I said. "Short for Frances." My voice to me sounded as scared as I suddenly felt.

This would be my life now, I realized, stuck in this small, bare room with two beds covered in matching plaid quilts, a desk, two reading lamps, a small closet, and a stranger. There was a window over the desk and I wanted to look out it to see what our view was, but at that moment, as Danny nodded curtly and turned her back to us again, I was afraid to move.

"Get your things unpacked," said Lill. "Then come to the great room and I'll show the two of you around the grounds."

I stood there, looking stupid and stunned. Lill said, "Anything else you need?"

When I didn't answer, she said, "Okay then," rubbed her hands together—a restless habit I would discover that she had—and left. Lill was the no-nonsense sister. She was most comfortable with a hammer, a drill or an ax in her hands. She carried a multi-tool in a leather holster on her belt and she was always fixing something.

I hadn't answered her because I'd lost my voice, an annoying thing that happened to me sometimes at the worst possible moments, a thing that used to frustrate Mom so much. As if I was doing it on purpose.

At the thought of Mom, I felt something slip inside me, like a car that stalls when it's stopped at a red light. I was okay as long as I was moving, but when something caused me to stop, it felt like getting going again might be impossible.

I pressed my legs against the bed just in time as they gave under me and I sat down heavily. The mattress squeaked underneath me.

"I left room for your suitcases up here," Danny said. She looked around the room. "It's small, but we won't be spending much time in here." Then she strode to the window and pulled back the curtain. "I can see the old fire tower from here. That's the first thing I want to check out."

I stared at her, trying to pull myself back from my thoughts of Mom.

"The new-wing rooms are a bit bigger, but I picked the old wing when I saw it this morning," she said. "More character. I'm glad they gave us a choice." She ran her foot over the polished wood floor. "I already know something about you."

My voice was still gone. I braced myself. Somehow she'd found out about Mom. She was going to ask me about it and I'd have to try to explain it without using the word *psychiatric*, which, believe me, is a word that in most people's minds means *crazy*, and if I say it, they take a step back, as if it's catching. I could just say she's in the hospital, which is true—she'd been there for months now—but then people ask what's wrong with her and I'm back to the same problem.

Danny continued moving around the room, opening the desk drawers (there were two), adjusting the gooseneck of the reading lamp on her side of the desk, checking under the bed (for what, I wasn't sure). Now she sat on her bed to lace up a pair of hiking boots.

Sweat seeped from my armpits and tingled on my upper lip and forehead, but a cold chill was making it hard to stop myself from shaking. I tried to steady my feet on the floor so Danny wouldn't notice.

I'd made a huge mistake. Without a phone, how would I contact Aunt Sissy? I couldn't even get internet to send an email until Sunday, a week away, because the school rules were that we could only go online on Sundays for an hour. It would probably take another week to hear back from Aunt Sissy and then more time for her to find a day when she wasn't in court to drive back out here from Vancouver to get me. It was unbearable. I'd die before then, of, I don't know, not being able to talk, or embarrassment, or loneliness, or maybe I wouldn't quite die for real but I'd die inside and I was already pretty close to that edge. I tried to breathe, but could only barely remember that I *could* breathe. *What have I done*, I thought.

I'd left my friends, the school where Mom used to be a counselor, what was left of my life. If I'd been old enough to live alone in a cabin in the woods, Grandma's cabin at Gem Lake, for instance, that's what I would have done. I'd thought maybe this would be close to that, surrounded by forest and mountains, and a fresh, cold creek that wound through the grounds and led deep into wilderness where I felt at home. I'd been told the school was small, only nine girls that year, and three of us were new that fall. But I hadn't thought about the questions I'd have to answer, and how I would explain myself.

Danny noticed my silence and turned to look at me with her steady brown eyes.

"I know you like the old wing better too," she said.

Relief washed over me like waves coming into shore, each one calming me a little. I managed to wipe my palms, which had been sweating, on my jeans.

The truth was, I'd only picked the old wing because I thought it would be cheaper. Aunt Sissy was paying my school tuition and I knew it was already costing her enough, exactly how much, I wasn't sure. She was too nice to tell me when I asked and only said, "Whatever it costs, it's worth it if you're happy." It was only later I found out that all the rooms cost the same amount.

My voice when I spoke was sticky. "This wing is eighty years old," I said, remembering what Lucy had told us when we visited in the summer. "It's the original part of the guest lodge." The walls of the original lodge were made of pine logs that had been fit tightly together and chinked with plaster. We could see the knots and cracks in the logs and the large beams that ran overhead. The floors were polished wood, only partly covered with multicolored woven rugs, and bearing the nicks and dents and scars of many years of use. When the sun dropped low in the sky in the afternoons, the wood glowed a soft, warm orange. The new wing was pretty too, brighter, with walls of a light, flat-paneled wood instead of log, and clean yellow linoleum floors. When we had visited in August, all the windows had been thrown open, gauzy white curtains billowing into the rooms from the fresh breeze through the window screens.

"There's a lot to explore," Danny said now. "Old buildings are always more interesting. Let's go see the fire tower. I'll help you put your stuff away."

That first evening at the school, we gathered in the great room for dinner. The room was open and airy. Solid pine beams spanned the width of the building. Paintings of birds and wildflowers hung on the walls. They'd been painted by Lill, who had gone to art school before becoming a teacher. She'd made the frames too, I found out later, of old cedar boards she'd salvaged from a shed that they'd torn down on the property.

My muscles tingled and I had some slivers; Danny and I had climbed the fire tower ladder several times, timing ourselves to see how fast we could get up and down. I sat down to eat at the long wooden table with eight other girls and the two sisters under the warm light from two chandeliers made of weathered white branches that hung from the beams. Smells of fresh-cut grass and ripe apples swept in through the open windows, along with the chirp of crickets.

"Did you know you can tell the temperature by the speed of crickets' chirping?" Lucy said into the burble of voices and clinking cutlery.

"Really?"

"It's getting cooler, so they're slower now."

"Count the number of chirps you hear in fourteen seconds," said Lill, raising her watch to check it. "I'll time, starting . . . now."

We sat listening and silently counting.

"Done," said Lill.

"I got thirty-one."

"Me too."

"I only got thirty."

"Close enough," said Lill. "Now you add forty and that gives you the temperature in Fahrenheit. About seventy degrees. What would it be in Celsius?"

"Subtract thirty and divide by two," said Lindsay. "So, something like twenty Celsius."

"Twenty-one," said Grace. "It's more accurate to subtract thirty-two and divide by one-point-eight."

"Okay," said Lill. "Good. You're right, Grace."

I felt what I hadn't felt in a long time: comfortable, even happy. I helped myself to a slice of warm bread that one of the girls had just taken from the oven. Nine girls sat around the table, passing around a big crock of rich stew made of moose meat, homegrown carrots and potatoes. By the time the snowstorm hit that November, there would only be eight girls. But on that warm summer evening, I could only think how glad I was to feel hungry again.

CHAPTER FOUR

Snow flung itself against the windows as we sat around the long pine table and listened to the storm sweeping in. Ms. B's spaghetti brought heat back to my toes and cheeks gradually.

"I don't know if the sisters are going to make it home tomorrow if this weather keeps up," Ms. B said.

"Can you stay?" said Jasie, the youngest girl. Like me and Danny, she was new to the school.

"Of course I'll stay," Ms. B said. "I don't think I have a choice." She laughed nervously.

"Don't worry," she added, seeing Jasie's frown. "Anyway, I'm sure they'll find a way to make it back. You know Lucy and Lill."

"Pass the salad, please," Danny said.

Just then a piercing shriek rang through the air like something had sheared loose in the wind. A deep, shuddering roar seemed to roll over the roof of the school like a wave. The next moment, we were plunged into darkness. Our gasps went up all at once.

It's funny how sounds seem to grow louder when you can't see anything six inches in front of your face. I hadn't noticed the way the wind moaned, slamming against the building like someone trying to get in. And I hadn't noticed the creaks and groans of the school's timbers or the high whistles where the storm found openings, reminding us we were no match for what it could bring. But in the dark, it all roared in my ears.

"Well, that's the power out," Ms. B said, her voice a little less bright than before.

"And the prize for stating the obvious goes to . . . ," someone said, which was a joke the girls often made, but which sounded ruder in the dark.

"Okay, okay," said Ms. B.

Something brushed against my leg, and then Lilac, the cat, was in my lap. I jumped and she pounced off, leaving the imprint of her claws in my thighs.

"What was that noise?" Jasie's voice squeaked out.

"It must have been the power line snapping," someone said, either Grace or Lindsay; I couldn't tell in the dark.

"I wonder if it was a tornado," said Jasie. "Are there tornadoes in winter?"

"I don't think we get tornadoes around here at any time of year," Ms. B said. "It's just a high wind, I think. Don't worry, girls. We're safe in this sturdy log building."

"I'll get the candles," I said. I knew where they were because I usually set the table and they were in the same drawer as the cloth napkins.

"Flashlights?" Ms. B said.

"I'll get them." Danny's voice.

It was so dark I had to feel my way along the wall, cross to the counter and feel for the end of the island. I fished in the drawer and heard the rattle of the wooden matches.

The match flared and as I touched it to the candlewick, everyone began to talk again at once.

"What about the emergency generator? Is it fixed yet?"

"No. Lill brought it into town. It's still there."

"We better fire up the woodstove."

"I wonder where the power lines went down."

"Probably a tree fell on it."

"How long will it take to fix?"

"The old wing is going to get cold tonight."

"Glad I'm in the new wing."

"Me too."

"I'm going to sleep in here, right by the woodstove," Jasie said.

"Let's all sleep in here. We can have a pajama party," Meredith said. "Oh no! My pie! It's not done yet."

Meredith spent her free time perfecting her baking skills. During her online hour on Sundays, she scanned the internet for recipes. We got to enjoy the benefits.

As I carried two candles to the table, a beam of light swept the room.

"Got the flashlights," Danny said. She was at the front door and shone the light out into the night. Snow was being driven sideways by the wind. A big gust tore the screen door from her hand and it clattered against the wall.

"Wow! The wind is crazy," she said, struggling to pull the door closed.

"Oh, there goes Lilac!" Jasie cried, as the cat darted past Danny and out into the storm. "Catch her!"

Jasie was the only girl in the school who didn't want to be there. On the first day around the dinner table, each of us had to introduce ourselves by telling a "first-day story" about what had brought us to the school. Jasie had said, "My mother's a triathlete and she runs hundred-day ultra-marathons through the wilderness and that's why I'm here, I guess. To make me stronger."

Not only was her mother an ultra-marathoner, but her dad was a competitive cyclist and both of them were doctors volunteering in Burkina Faso, a place in Africa I'd never even heard of until she told us about it. Jasie said her parents' families had both come from small villages in India. They wanted to help people who were growing up in places like their families had come from. "I grew up in Calgary," Jasie said. "They think I need to toughen up. But it's not going to work. I'm hopeless."

"I'm hopeless" was Jasie's favorite saying. She said it when we went on a hike and she forgot her water bottle, and she said it when we took a first aid course and were learning the Heimlich maneuver. She was practicing on Danny and she sprained her wrist. She said it so often, it became a little bit true, although I hate to say that about her.

She's a sweet girl. Dad used to say I was eighty-five pounds soaking wet. Jasie wouldn't be that on a good day. She had a delicate, worried face like a nervous bird and she barely ate enough to keep a frog alive. Even now, I could see in the candlelight her plate of spaghetti barely touched, her fork dropped mid-bite. She liked to push her food around her plate, to try and make it look like she'd eaten more than she had, and that's what it looked like now, all heaped on the edges.

Danny had slipped on a pair of rubber boots that were always by the front door and now she was out in the snow, trying to catch Lilac.

"Don't worry," Meredith said, patting Jasie's arm. "She'll catch her. You know Danny."

"No she won't," Jasie said, her voice trembling.

I was afraid she was right. Lilac loved to be carried around (mainly by Jasie) and she slept on the bed of whoever left their bedroom door ajar (mainly Jasie), but she loved even more to be outside. Escaping outside after supper was one of her favorite games. Sometimes she carried tiny mice held gently in her mouth into the school and released them, live. In nice weather, it could be grasshoppers or moths. The sisters warned us to be careful when we went in and out. If the cat got out at night and we couldn't get her back in, she could be carried off by a coyote or even a big eagle or owl.

Tonight the added worry was the snowstorm. If we couldn't find her before bedtime, she'd be out overnight in the cold and snow.

I heard Jasie's sniffles and then turned and saw, in the candlelight, big tears rolling down her cheeks as she sat stock-still and tried to pretend she wasn't crying.

Ms. B got up and went to the front door. She opened it and drew a sharp breath as the wind blasted in. "Danielle!" she called. "Come in and finish your supper. The cat can look after herself." I knew that Ms. B wasn't only worried about Danny finishing supper. I could feel her nervousness rising with the worsening storm.

After a minute, Danny appeared, her hair and clothes rimmed with snow. She stomped her boots on the mat then pulled them off.

"She doesn't want to come. I could see her eyes looking at me from under the porch. Sorry, Jasie. I didn't think she'd run out in this weather."

We finished supper quietly by the flickering candlelight as the storm grew even fiercer. Every once in a while, the wind tossed something against the house and Ms. B tried not to look nervous, but failed, her face alert and listening for trouble. All of us listened.

With Jasie's quiet tears in the soft darkness, maybe all of the girls felt, as I did, a little more lonely than usual.

"Help me get Lilac back in?" Danny said, after we'd piled the dirty dinner dishes beside the sink to wash once the power came back on.

"Jasie won't sleep tonight if we don't," I said.

We both knew that was true. But we also knew that we'd need a good story if Ms. B was going to let us go out in the snowstorm tonight.

We went to ask her together. When Ms. B called Danny *Danielle*, she didn't even correct her. We nodded and agreed to be back in half an hour, whether we'd caught Lilac or not. We stuck flashlights in our pockets. Jasie handed me a can of cat food and a fork.

"Tap on the side of the can," she said. "That usually brings her running."

I was thinking she was unlikely to hear it above the roar of the wind, but I took them from her and I smiled into Jasie's worried face to try and reassure her.

The other girls were bringing their blankets and pillows into the great room and spreading them in front of the fireplace that cast a warm orange glow on the walls.

"My pie isn't done," Meredith called from the kitchen. "But I'll try to finish it in the woodstove oven. I'll make hot chocolate!"

Danny and I put on our boots, waved, and plunged into the storm. Once the door was closed firmly and we had left behind that cozy room, a fizz of excitement bubbled through me. The mystery of the storm pulled us in, the bite of wind, a curtain of snow across a world of possibility.

"Lilac!" I called out. Then I burst out laughing, and so did Danny. The wind had snatched my voice and it was lost in the whining gusts. Calling her was useless.

Danny squatted and shone her flashlight under the porch. "I don't see her!" she shouted.

"She likes the shed at the end of the driveway!" I shouted back.

Danny took my arm and we leaned into the wind, our flashlights beaming a halo into the driving snow.

At the end of the driveway, we ducked into the shed. The thin walls made a six-foot by six-foot cube of calm where we caught our breath. Snow clung to the hair around our faces. Lilac was not there.

"This is crazy," said Danny.

"Trees will come down tonight for sure."

"Let's walk down the road and see if we can see what caused the power outage."

"What about Lilac?"

"I bet she's hiding out somewhere near the house. We can hurry."

I checked my watch. "We've got exactly twenty-one minutes."

A few minutes down the road, a shadowy bulk rose out of the white blur. As we got closer, I realized the blur was a huge pine tree that had fallen across the road. It had brought down the power line, which had snapped and now lay snaked in the snow and tangled among the pine branches.

But the strange thing was that in the woods beyond the fallen tree, a swath of trees had been pushed partway over. They were leaning on each other, like they'd been pushed by a giant hand. Could it have been a tornado?

Danny and I stood staring at it, puzzled.

"Is that what they call a blow-down?" Danny asked, her voice catching on the wind.

"I've never seen anything like that," I answered.

"It had to be some freak wind pattern," said Danny. "Or aliens."

The wind blasted up the road, rocking our bodies as we tried to stay in place.

"We've got nine minutes to get back and find Lilac," Danny shouted.

We ran up the road with the wind at our backs this time, almost lifting us off our feet. Near the school, I got out the can of cat food and the fork and I sang Lilac's name into the night.

Her orange-and-black head appeared from under the porch and she bounded to the front door before us.

"Lucky!" said Danny. I looked at my watch. As we opened the door, it had been half an hour on the dot.

CHAPTER FIVE

The great room was aglow with candles burning in lanterns placed on bookshelves and tables. Jasie jumped up and ran to scoop Lilac into her arms. She buried her face in the cat's fur. The tears still ran down her cheeks, even though Lilac was found.

She's homesick, I thought, but I couldn't think of anything to say to make her feel better. Stepping into the warm homeyness of the school, a tide of homesickness washed over me, too. The girls lay on their stomachs on sleeping bags and blankets in front of the fireplace. Ms. B sat at the dining room table with her knitting bag. She had brought the transistor radio from the kitchen and extended the antenna its full length. The station she'd picked up was not quite tuned in; a staticky voice faded in and out.

"This fire is so mesmerizing," Meredith said from the nest of sleeping bags in front of the fireplace.

"It's our own fireplace channel," Carmen said. "Sorry, you two, we used all the air mattresses. If you want to sleep here, you'll have to sleep on the floor."

"You snooze, you lose," said Grace. "Wilderness survival rule number twenty-seven."

On the day that everyone had introduced themselves around the dining room table, Grace had said, "I'm the girl who's hard to like." That had had the reverse effect of making me determined to prove I could like her. But she didn't make it easy.

"I just say what's on my mind," she'd continued. "Apparently, that's not what you do if you want people to like you. Honestly, I don't care if you like me or not. If you do something stupid, I'm probably going to say so."

"She means it," Meredith had said. Meredith was in eleventh grade with Grace and Lindsay, the girls who'd been there from the first year.

Lucy, with a strained look on her face, had smiled and said, "Thank you, Grace. Who would like to go next?"

Taking another piece of bread from the stack on the table, Grace had added, "It's nothing personal. You might as well get used to it. Pass me the butter. Oh, and the sisters are my step-aunts."

Meredith told us later that after Lucy and Lill's mother died, their father remarried, to a woman who already had a daughter of her own. A few years after the marriage when the daughter, Grace's mom, was in her late teens, she took off. She'd gone missing for many years, and when she showed up again she had a child of her own and nowhere to live. She and Grace had lived with Lucy and Lill's father and his wife, and then eventually she disappeared again, leaving Grace behind. Because of that, Grace attended Green Mountain Academy tuition-free, which was too bad, Meredith said, because the school needed all the paying students it could get.

Grace also had crazy good carpentry skills. She'd built a copy of the desks in the bedrooms of the old wing for her room in the new wing, complete with the two drawers and legs that were as graceful as fawn's legs. I thought hers was nicer than the originals. Lindsay said Grace had added a secret compartment in hers. She'd also built a miniature gazebo for the mice that sometimes scurried along the porch railing. She left little pieces of cheese and peanut butter crackers in there for them. No one could be sure if mice ever used it, although something ate the food she left. And she'd built a bench, for one person, in the front yard with a roof over it and a bird condominium a few feet away on a pole, so when she sat on the bench, she could watch the birds. Technically, anyone could sit on the bench. But no one else ever did.

Grace said she couldn't build something unless it came from her own mind. She turned down requests for bookshelves. Too boring, she said. She liked a challenge. She had, though, retooled the winter sleds so that a set of wheels could be attached to them, or taken off, depending on the trail conditions. In October, we'd used those sleds for hauling the wood that Lill had cut up when she cleared trails.

"Who wants popcorn?" Ming called now.

"I'll help you make it," Danny said.

We kicked off our boots and put them to dry on the rack by the woodstove.

"Is it too warm in here?" said Ms. B, fanning herself with her knitting instructions.

It *was* warm, with both the woodstove and the fireplace fully stoked. But the heat and the light they threw was comforting against the deepening cold and howling wind outside. I checked the thermometer: minus eight degrees Celsius. It would get colder through the night. A good supply of wood lay stacked neatly near the fireplace, but we would burn through that quickly.

The original two-story building had had two additions over the years: first the great room and kitchen, then the new wing with classrooms and more bedrooms. Without power, all the heat came from the woodstoves in the kitchen and great room. The rooms in the old wing, where Danny and I had our bedroom, would be drafty and cold. The upstairs rooms weren't used for sleeping anymore; one was a storeroom and the others had been stripped of their plaster, with a middle wall knocked down. They were going to be made into a big art studio, eventually. The more I got to know the school, and the sisters, the more I realized that a lot of things were going to happen "eventually." Lucy and Lill had plans, but, apparently, not money. I knew that the trip they'd made this weekend had to do with trying to find a way to keep the school going.

"Oh, listen!" Ms. B suddenly cried. She turned up the radio.

"Search and rescue crews are looking for a small aircraft that took off from Penticton Airport this afternoon and disappeared on its way to Seattle, according to Canadian Coast Guard officials. The plane was expected to land in Seattle at 5 p.m., but it never arrived. Three people were on board the single-engine Piper Cherokee aircraft. A search for the white plane with red and navy striping has been temporarily called off, due to deteriorating weather. Search officials believe the plane may have been en route back to Penticton airport due to weather conditions at the time of its disappearance."

"How awful!" said Ms. B. "On a night like this."

I felt the curious gazes of the other girls slowly swing and land on me. My cheeks flushed under their stares. By now, they all knew the story of my dad, who had walked out to get help when our truck broke down and we got stranded on a road in, as Mom called it, "the middle of nowhere." It was actually a logging road in Oregon, and technically, we knew exactly where we were. The road just wasn't on our map.

Our story had ended up in newspapers all over the United States and Canada. A big picture of me, looking like a startled raccoon, flanked every story. A newspaper reporter had snapped it when I came out of the hospital with Aunt Sissy on a warm sunny day in May, a beautiful day, except for the fact that my life had changed forever. The newspapers and even TV stations, when they told the story, usually showed that picture of me, along with one of our old red truck, what was left of it, on Red Fox Road. If you do a Google search of my name, Francie Fox, you can find those photos in newspapers from Fernie, British Columbia, to Florida.

Aunt Sissy wouldn't let reporters interview me. "It's disrespectful," she said. "Under the circumstances."

Actually, when we'd first gotten stranded, I had daydreamed about being on the news, for some heroic thing I'd done—fixing our truck with a coat hanger and duct tape or something like that, and then driving it out myself, taking everybody to safety. They say be careful what you wish for. I say, be specific.

❖

Danny had gone to our room and brought back our sleeping bags and pillows. She spread them out side by side, next to Ming and Jasie. Ms. B, who seemed sorry she'd listened to the news, had turned the radio off and sat knitting in the candlelight. When we were all lying in our bags—the bigger girls, Grace and Lindsay and Carmen, on their elbows staring into the crackling fire—Ms. B said, "Aren't we lucky? Safe inside on a night like this. Tomorrow the power will come back on and everything will go back to normal."

We were all quiet for a minute and then Grace said, "Or it might not. Last year when the power went out, it was off for three days. The generator didn't work then either."

"Well okay," said Ms. B. "Anyway, we're safe here. We're well-equipped for any eventuality."

I stared up at the ceiling beams and tried to think of what "normal" would be like now. No one was living in our house in Penticton. Grandpa went by every week to check on it, pick up any mail, and turn on different lights so it looked lived in. I couldn't even imagine how weird it must be—the sunlight slanting through the side door and falling across the bare dining room table. There would probably be dust, although Aunt Sissy paid someone to dust and vacuum once a month. How dirty does an empty house get? I pictured the glow-in-the-dark stars I had glued on my bedroom ceiling in the shape of the Big Dipper.

Suddenly the loneliness that had been lapping at the edges of my heart welled up and threatened to knock me down. I shook off my sleeping bag and got up. Danny gave me a look that said, "Are you okay?" but she didn't say anything.

I took a flashlight and went down the hall to our bedroom.

Under my bed, I stored a box of things from our house that I'd wanted to keep with me—a shimmery stone I'd found on a hike at Gem Lake and that Dad said might have gold in it; Dad's blue-and-red Canada Post toque; an amber necklace that had belonged to Grandma; a framed picture of Mom and me and Phoebe, Mom in the middle, holding our hands, on our first day of kindergarten. It had hung on the wall in my bedroom at home, but I couldn't bear to hang it on the wall here and be reminded every day.

My twin sister Phoebe was gone. She was dead, a word I still found hard to say sometimes. If I didn't think too hard, I could remember the smell of her, sweet and milky, like clover. I could remember the way she could make me laugh so hard I'd pee my pants, and how that made us laugh even more. Once, I laughed so hard, I threw up. We'd been sitting under a curtain of grape vines eating purple grapes, so it came out pink. But if I thought too much, I remembered things I didn't want to remember, like the pale bluish color of her eyelids as she lay on the grass at Gem Lake and how her eyes wouldn't open, though I shook her shoulder. And then, if I wanted to feel even worse, I could remember Mom shaking me, yelling at me that she had warned me not to chase Phoebe because of her heart condition. It was that day our family began to unravel, first one thread, then another, pulling apart the world I'd known so well.

I took out the photo album. I had learned to look at the photo album only when I was already so homesick, it wouldn't matter. I sat on the bed and turned to a page near the beginning—a picture of all of us—Mom, Dad, Phoebe and me. Phoebe and I were about six years old. We're sitting at the picnic table on the beach at Gem Lake, where Grandma's cabin was—still is, though no one goes there anymore. The sun is sparkling on the lake in the background. All of us are smiling, but Mom is laughing, maybe at something the person behind the camera has said. It's the best picture I have of Phoebe, the one that looks like the Phoebe I remember. It's also the best one I have of Mom—the way I'd like to remember her. It would be a long time before Mom smiled again.

That was our family. Was. A shiver ran through my body. I reached for a corner of the quilt and pulled it over my shoulders. It was already getting cold in this wing. I noticed a sound that had been there for a while, but that my brain hadn't quite made sense of. Something was banging repeatedly in a room above ours.

I put the photo album back in the box and shoved it under my bed. Then I guided myself down the hall with the flashlight.

We weren't allowed to go up to the second floor rooms in the old wing, because the rooms were being renovated and the sisters said there were exposed wires and other hazards. Lucy sometimes went up there to work, and the older girls said you could get internet up there, so I guessed that some of them had sneaked up.

There was only one other room where you could get internet in the school, a classroom in the new wing. Lill made a schedule every Monday after supper for our hour of time by drawing names from a hat. Having no internet most of the time was part of the school's philosophy; that's what Lucy and Lill had explained to Aunt Sissy and me on our first visit. If we wanted, we could look things up in the big set of encyclopedias and dictionaries or the many other reference books kept on shelves in the classroom.

"Old-school. Literally," Lill had said and winked at me.

"What about emergencies?" Aunt Sissy had asked.

"We drive out," Lucy had said. "It's important that parents—um—guardians, understand that. We both have extensive first aid training. But we're an hour's drive from medical help."

"What do you think, Francie?" Aunt Sissy had asked.

I'd only been half-listening. I'd been staring out the window at a path I could see curving into the woods. Bright green leaves shimmered in the sun and cast shifting shadows on the earth. It looked so inviting and mysterious. I wondered what was around the bend.

"About what?" I said.

"About no internet."

"It's okay with me," I said. "Mom and Dad don't let me have a phone."

Danny and I had planned to sneak upstairs to the second floor ourselves some night. We thought we might be able to send signals using a flashlight from the fire tower to one of the upstairs windows, but so far we hadn't found the opportunity to get into the rooms up there.

In the hall, the wind whimpered like a small, trapped animal, coming from everywhere and nowhere, sighing through the nooks and crannies of the old wing. I started up the stairs. They creaked under my feet. In the stairwell, the whimpering was even louder, rising to a cry, then dropping again. I hesitated, then took another step. It was only the wind. But shadows danced on the walls in the light cast from my flashlight. My own shadow looked like a hunched old woman creeping along.

As I reached the room over our bedroom, I felt a gust of cold air scurrying along the floor. It whistled under the closed door. I turned the door handle and shoved the door open.

Bang! The sound made me jump, even though in my flashlight beam I could see what it was—a window was swinging on its hinge, being caught by the wind and then slammed shut every few seconds. I swept the beam of light around the room. A polished wood floor shone in the light. Against one wall, below the window, was a desk with a laptop computer on it.

Papers had been blown all over the floor. At the far end of the room, chairs were stacked on top of round tables. Several folded-up cots leaned against the wall. They were probably left over from the time when the school was a lodge.

Snow had sifted in on the windowsill and the desk. I went to the window. As I reached out to pull it closed, a blast of wind slapped snow in my face. Three people were lost out there in the billowing snow and deepening cold. Could they have landed their airplane somewhere to ride out the storm? How much space did a small plane need to land? This area was just miles and miles of forested mountains.

There was a small weedy lake a few kilometers to the east that we called Swamp Thing Lake. The sisters had named it when they were younger. A rough untended trail led to it. All of us girls had hiked there on a hot day in September with Lill. Some of us had waded into the lake to cool off, but only Jasie had picked up about twenty leeches, clinging to her ankles and twined between her toes. "I'm hopeless," she had said.

I didn't think Swamp Thing Lake would be big enough to land on, at least not without hitting a lot of trees first. If I were the pilot, what would I do? The only clear area in all that bush might be a road. Yes, I'd aim for a road, I thought, try to use it as a little runway. If they landed somewhere, they'd be in for a long, cold night. There could be injuries, too. But if they didn't land . . . I shivered.

The window latch was broken, but I fastened it as well as I could and hoped the wind wouldn't pull it open again. Then I bent to gather the papers that had been scattered across the floor. As I bent over, an eerie blue light suddenly illuminated the polished floor. A squeal escaped from me before I could help it. But as I stood, I saw that it was only Lucy's laptop screen that had lit up. It would be running on battery. I must have knocked the mouse and woken it up.

Stupid to be so jumpy. There was nothing to be scared of.

I stacked the papers neatly and put them on the chair. Then I used my sleeve to brush the snow off the desk. The laptop was open to an email message. Obviously, I shouldn't look at it. Reading someone else's email was not okay, as Mom and Dad had reminded me when I read Mom's once, from the principal at our school. Dad, who is—*was*, I guess—a mail carrier for Canada Post, had said that reading email was just like picking up mail off someone's porch and slicing it open, which I didn't think was a fair comparison. It was more like reading a letter that was already open and had been left lying in plain view on the kitchen table.

The thing was, a word in Lucy's email had caught my eye: *irresponsible*. I could just close the laptop, but then she might wonder why I'd done that. Or I could just walk away.

I snuck another look.

It's really irresponsible for you and Lill to hold us hostage to this crazy scheme of yours. It's been crazy from the start. It's a money pit. A black hole of expenses. Did you really think girls would want to go to school in the middle of nowhere? And you realize, I hope, that Grace is part of the problem???

Three question marks. Even if I hadn't been able to see the name on the screen, it was obvious who had written this. Larry Larsen, Lucy and Lill's brother. They had another brother, too, named Luke. The two of them had been at the school last month and there were a lot of triple question marks then, too—angry voices behind closed doors.

We had first heard this story from Meredith, who'd been at the school since it opened.

"The brothers live in Toronto," she'd said. "All four of them inherited the lodge, but only Lucy and Lill wanted to live here. The brothers want to build a luxury resort out here, with multiple buildings, a spa, a tennis court, a swimming pool and a heli-pad. We'll be lucky if the school lasts until the end of the school year. They're deep in debt."

"What's deepindebt?" Jasie had asked, and the older girls laughed.

"Debt is when you owe a lot of money," Meredith said.

"It means you can't pay your bills," Ming added. "Sometimes people lose their homes."

"Would that mean I could go home?" Jasie said.

"Why would you want to leave us?" Meredith said. "We're like your sisters now. The big sisters you never even knew you wanted."

I could see part of what Lucy had written, too, in the message before Larry's: *You know Mom wouldn't have wanted that. We're looking for ideas to bring in more students. We'll know more after this weekend.*

To read any more, I'd have to click on something or scroll down. I felt guilty enough already. It wasn't a secret that the school was in trouble. Meredith had said, "Let's face it. There aren't that many girls who think it's a great idea to spend ten months of the year in the middle of nowhere with no boys and no phone."

"It's just a crazy few!" Ming added. She had grinned, thrown an arm around Jasie and flipped Jasie's thick braid.

I stared out at the snow swirling across the yard, and at the tall trees tossing and bending. Then I made my decision. I put my finger on the mouse and scrolled down a little more. Larry's message carried on: *This is your last chance. At the end of this year, there'll be no more money. I'm not putting a penny more into this fiasco. It's time to close this operation down and send the kids home in time for Christmas.*

I couldn't believe it. By Christmas? It was already November. I couldn't go home, not now. Danny was the best friend I'd ever had. Nobody got me like Danny got me. And if I left now I'd have to live with Grandpa and his moods. Or worse, I'd have to move to the city to live with Aunt Sissy. I couldn't survive if I couldn't get outside to the woods every day. I'd go crazy.

The panic swirled inside me like the storm, kicking up all my fears. I had a flash of what it would be like to be inside that small airplane, tossed around in the storm, unable to find a safe place to land.

As a whirlwind of snow pummeled the window, rattling it, I felt sick. I had to tell Danny. There had to be something we could do. I closed the door on the room and hurried along the hall to the stairs. A window on the landing cast a ghostly glow on the opposite wall. This old lodge must have seen many storms as bad as this, I thought.

Downstairs, another flashlight beam was coming along the dark hall toward me.

"Francie! Where were you? I was looking for you."

"Danny, you won't believe what I just found."

"Where were you? Did you go upstairs?"

"How did you even know that?"

"I just had a feeling. You did, didn't you?"

"I heard a noise. I didn't think about it."

"You didn't think to tell me you were going up to the room we've been wanting to get into all fall?"

"Okay, I'm sorry. Listen, this is more important. I saw an email."

I told her what I'd read.

"That can't happen," Danny said. "We just got here. I have plans."

"There's got to be something we can do," I said.

"Poor Grace," said Danny.

"Poor Grace? Really?"

"Larry said she's part of the problem. It's true. She's her own worst enemy. You can see how mad she gets at herself."

"You're more observant than I am, I guess," I said.

"Well, that's probably true." Danny smiled. "But didn't you notice what she did for our hike the other day?"

"Nearly biting Jasie's head off, you mean?"

"Before that. She *volunteered* to partner with Jasie."

"That's true. That was weird, considering."

"Not really. She's trying."

We'd been eating breakfast and arranging the partners for our hike.

"Teams of two," Lucy said. "Should we draw names?"

"I'll go with Jasie," Grace said, then she gave a sideways look to see if Lill had noticed. She had. She'd nodded her approval.

"She's trying her best to make up for the Soleil incident," Danny said now. "The school can't afford to lose any more girls. That's what Larry meant in his email. Grace's temper is a big pain for the sisters. Everybody knows it."

"She doesn't have a temper, exactly."

"You're right. See, you are observant."

"She just speaks her thoughts out loud. Which you'd think would be normal."

Grace's thoughts, when we hiked out into the middle of thick bush with a chill wind coming off the cliffs, and she discovered that Jasie had forgotten to pick up their lunches off the kitchen counter, were: "Can you not get one thing straight? How hard is it? You had one job—to carry the lunches."

Jasie's eyes had filled up and she'd stood with her fists balled at her sides, just taking it. As tears spilled over onto her cheeks she'd whispered, "I'm hopeless."

"And can you please please stop saying that?" Grace had added. "It doesn't solve anything."

"She was right," I said to Danny. "It was a bad mistake."

"Lill reamed Grace out later. Her whole plan to be nice totally backfired."

"But what are we going to do about the school?" I said.

"Maybe I'll email Mom about it on Sunday," Danny said. Danny's mom was chief financial officer of their First Nation. Danny told me her mom was happiest sitting at the dining room table with stacks of paper, a cup of coffee, and her laptop open to spreadsheets full of numbers. "She knows about all that financial stuff."

"Well, I don't know about that. Won't that make her have doubts? What if she pulls you out of the school?"

"She knows how much I wanted to come here. I begged her for a year. I don't think she'll change her mind."

"But she could, couldn't she?"

"You worry too much, Francie."

A bang overhead made us both jump and clutch each other's hand. Something had slammed into the roof. Whatever it was rolled along it in a series of thumps and cracks that made the building shudder.

Ms. B came rushing down the hall, followed by the crowd of girls, all talking at once.

"What was that?"

"It had to be a tree."

"It sounded like it crashed right through the roof."

"I'm scared."

"Listen, you can still hear it. It's scratching against the roof."

"I've been here the longest and I've never seen a storm like this before," said Grace.

"Everyone back to their sleeping bags," said Ms. B.

"We should investigate," said Grace.

"No one is going outside," Ms. B said. "Not in these conditions."

"We could check upstairs," I said.

"And what do we do if there's a hole in the roof?"

"A hole in the roof is the last thing this school needs," said Grace. Everyone turned to look at her.

"I'm just saying. We can't afford to fix the generator. You think we can afford a new roof?"

"Okay," said Ms. B. "Let's all try to be helpful if we can."

"I don't get how that's unhelpful. It's just a fact."

"We can do without your kind of facts," Meredith said.

"My kind of facts? Like there's a kind of facts?"

"Yeah, your specialty is the kind of facts that make people feel bad," Meredith said.

"Facts or no facts," Ms. B said, "we're going to stay down here where it's safe. No one goes anywhere."

CHAPTER SIX

Everyone knew that Meredith was talking about "the Soleil incident," as Danny called it.

Soleil was the ninth girl around the great room table on the first day of September. She had a head of yellow-white curls fuzzed around her face, and when she stood in the sunlight, or even near a bright lamp, her hair glowed like a halo. She rarely smiled, but when she did, it was like you'd won a prize.

"I like to draw," Soleil said when her turn came to tell her first-day story. Her face came up and caught the light as she spoke. "Mostly birds," she added. Then she bent her head again. She was done.

Lill said, "And you live in Victoria. I hear you're a kayaker."

"Yes," said Soleil, not raising her head.

Lill gave it another try. "Grace draws, too."

"I don't draw birds," Grace said. "I draw useful things."

The more Lill tried to help Soleil fit in, the worse it was.

"Don't force it," I heard Lucy say to Lill one evening as I carried the supper dishes into the kitchen. "She'll find her way. Just let her."

But Lill liked to fix things—and not just squeaky hinges and lights that flickered. Lucy said if Lill wasn't on a ladder, she was under something: a sink, a vehicle, the porch where the wasps made their nests. Soleil became one of her fix-it projects.

One warm Sunday morning in late September as we ate breakfast, Lill said, "I saw a mountain bluebird near the bench earlier. You could take your sketchbook out there, Soleil."

Soleil's face momentarily lit up.

"Is that the bird in the painting?" She gestured with her chin to the painting that hung between the windows near the dining table. It was the most beautiful of all the paintings in the school—a delicately shaded mountain bluebird perched on a fencepost, its chest feathers going from radiant blue and fading into pale white, and a single sprig of yellow grass crossing the background.

Her question was the most we'd heard her say in a single sitting since she'd arrived.

"She can't use the bench," Grace burst out. "I'm fixing it."

"Fixing it? What's wrong with it?" Lill asked.

"There are wasps," Grace said. "And one of the boards is loose. Besides, I was going to sit out there myself."

Lill took a deep breath and cleared her throat. She always did that when she was annoyed.

"All right," she said. "Then Grace, you can take Soleil out to Swamp Thing Lake. That's the best place to see bird life this time of year."

"Why do I have to take her?" Grace asked. "Shouldn't someone who likes her take her?"

Lill threw down her napkin and shoved her chair back as she rose from the table. "Can we talk in the kitchen please, Grace?"

Soleil looked like she wanted the floor to open and swallow her. She put down her half-eaten toast and worked at making her napkin into a perfect triangle.

"Lindsay and I are taking our bikes down the road later," Ming said. "You can come with us, Soleil."

But Lill was determined to teach Grace a lesson. So after breakfast, Soleil tucked her sketchbook and pencils into her backpack, put on her boots and followed Grace out the door.

Sundays were free days, and Lucy and Lill only made us follow one rule: make sure someone knows where you're going. Danny and I had our internet hour after breakfast, but neither of us ever took the full time. We were done in fifteen minutes and we packed lunches to take to the Sasquatch Caves.

As we got our boots on by the door, Grace came back in, alone.

"Where's Soleil?" Meredith asked, coming from the kitchen.

"I left her at the lake," Grace said. "She doesn't talk much, in case you didn't notice. I didn't see any point in staying."

"I wonder what Lill will say."

"Why would you wonder that? Don't you have anything more interesting to think about?" Grace grabbed her tool bag and went back outside.

Danny and I spent the afternoon at the Sasquatch Caves. On our way back, some clouds scudded across the sky, blocking the sun, and the wind picked up, cooling the air. Our light jackets, which had been more than we needed in the morning, weren't quite warm enough. The nip in the air made it good to come inside. A fire popped and roared in the woodstove and the smell of Lucy's vegetable curry mingled with the woodsmoke. The chill had brought everyone back from their outings. Except Soleil.

"Where's Soleil?" Lill asked, coming in just behind us. She held the cordless drill and a tin of screws. As usual, she had been fixing something.

"We didn't see her," Danny said.

"Grace?" Lill called to where she sat at the dining table with a ruler and a graph paper, drawing a plan for something.

"Last I saw her she was at the lake," Grace said.

"Ming, take someone else and go look for Soleil." She took her drill and went down to the basement.

"I'll go," said Danny.

"I'll come, too," I said.

As we put on warmer jackets, Grace, without looking up from her drawing, said, "She was going to the south end."

"The south end?"

"Is there an echo in here?" Grace said.

"The south end where the quicksand is, you mean?" Ming asked.

Grace didn't answer. She erased something from her drawing and blew the crumbs off the page.

"Let's go," Ming said.

We took the trail at a quick jog.

"What's the quicksand?" I asked.

"We never go to the south end of the lake because if it's been wet, the mud is like quicksand. You can't even get to the shore. You'll sink to your knees before that."

We'd been hiking about twenty minutes when we saw Soleil coming toward us through the trees. Her feet were bare and coated in thick black mud that went halfway up her legs. Patches of it had dried on her face and her T-shirt was streaked with it.

"Take my jacket," Ming said, stripping it off and helping Soleil into it. "You're shivering."

She put Soleil's backpack on her own back and said, "Francie, you and Soleil head back to the school. Danny and I will go get Soleil's boots."

"You won't find them," Soleil said.

"We'll find them. Don't worry. Now get going."

We hurried back to the school and let ourselves in the back door.

"Don't tell anyone," Soleil said.

"I won't. I'll take you upstairs and run a bath for you."

Soleil's room was in the new wing, so it was easy enough to go up the back stairs without anyone seeing us.

"Did you see any birds?"

"I saw a great blue heron. I was trying to get closer to it," Soleil said through chattering teeth.

"I'll knock on your door when the bath is ready."

Her green eyes when she looked at me were full of tears, but she turned away quickly without saying anything more.

As I ran the bath in the shared bathroom down the hall, I thought how it could have been funny. Maybe if it hadn't been done intentionally, maybe if it had happened to me or to Danny, it would have been a funny story to tell at dinner. But it was Soleil, and Grace had done it to be mean. So it wasn't funny.

I didn't tell anyone, and neither did Ming or Danny. Danny cleaned Soleil's boots, which she'd gotten to by laying dead branches across the quicksand, and no one asked questions about why the boots were drying by the woodstove. It was normal to see an assortment of footwear by the stove at the end of the day with the laces loosened and the tongues pulled out, draped over the drying rack Lill had made out of coat hangers.

At dinner, Lucy and Carmen, who were both singers, had chattered about where they should bring in the harmony on the song they were learning together and whether it should be high or low harmony. They had made us join in as they tried it, though neither Grace nor Soleil nor Lill did, I noticed. Soleil kept her eyes on her plate, as she usually did, and when Lucy asked her about what birds she'd seen at Swamp Thing Lake, she'd said, "A great blue heron." And those were the last four words any of us heard her speak.

Two days later Lill helped Soleil put her bags in the back of the SUV. We waved from the porch and Soleil briefly raised her hand at the car window, then faced straight ahead to the road taking her back to town.

CHAPTER SEVEN

Danny had said the storm would get crazy and she was right.
Ms. B wouldn't let us go outside to investigate what had hit the
roof, but from the window we could see that a big, broken tree
limb had tumbled across the lawn to rest near the porch.

"That's probably from the cottonwood near the end of the
driveway," Lindsay said. "That poor old tree. It's over a hundred
years old, but it's sure taken a beating."

The cottonwood's trunk was so big, Danny and I couldn't
circle it with our arms, even with our hands linked. Limbs
had already broken off or died, and flickers used holes in them
for homes.

"Come away from the windows," Ms. B called. "You're
making me nervous."

"We're safe in here," Lindsay said. "Don't worry."

Ms. B sat back down with her knitting and turned the radio
on again.

Meredith, wearing an apron and oven mitts, brought her
pie over and set it on the stone hearth in front of the fire.

"It's a little crispy, but I think it will still taste good," she said.

She had finished baking it in a small compartment on the side of the woodstove. One side was browner than the other, but it smelled delicious.

"What about ice cream?" Grace said.

"I'm on it," said Lindsay, jumping up.

We ate the crispy pie while watching the fire.

I knew we were safe, but I couldn't stop thinking about the missing plane and the three people on it. I had a feeling that I couldn't shake, something I was on the edge of seeing but that wouldn't quite come into focus.

"Oh, turn it up!" Carmen suddenly cried. She jumped up with her fork in her fist.

"Catch Me" was on the radio. All the girls in the school had the song on their phones and we played it while we did indoor chores. Even Lucy and Lill loved it.

"Just because you see me run, doesn't mean you're not the one," she sang into her fork microphone.

"Catch me!" We all joined in on the chorus. It was impossible to resist. Meredith pulled Jasie to her feet and they danced in front of the fireplace. Ming and Lindsay did the backup vocals.

"Who sings this?" Ms. B asked, laughing.

No one answered. We knew all the words and we had to sing them all.

"Oh, I hate when they do that!" Carmen cried as the radio announcer's voice cut in just before the last note. "They need to let the song finish."

"You've really never heard of Diamond Lee?" Grace said to Ms. B. "She's only the biggest singer in Canada right now. Maybe North America."

"Well, this isn't my usual radio station," she said, smiling.

Everyone settled back to their blankets on the floor. For three minutes, Jasie had forgotten to be lonely, I had forgotten to think about the missing plane, and Grace and Meredith had forgotten to be mad at each other.

But as soon as we were quiet again, my mind remembered the little fire I kept smoldering in my heart and I piled on more worried thoughts to get it burning again. I had not seen Mom since Dad was found. Aunt Sissy had written a long email explaining what Mom's doctor had said and why Aunt Sissy decided not to come and get me. She used words like *shock* and *unfortunate* and wrote that her response was *not expected*, words I spent a long time trying to decipher. I couldn't help thinking that if Mom had wanted to see me, Aunt Sissy would have come out to get me right away.

Not that I wanted to go to the city. In my dream, Mom comes to see me. I show her the fire tower and the creek where kokanee salmon run in the fall. I sit with her beside the trembling aspens, their yellow leaves shimmering with life. I knew that if Mom came out here, she would want to live again. There was nothing in that drab, chemical-smelling hospital ward that would make anyone want to live.

I don't think it was just me who was remembering something. I felt the let-down in the room, even from Ms. B.

Meredith clapped her hands as if to chase it away. "We should sing some camp songs!" she said.

Grace groaned. "Don't you ever get tired?"

"The other day," Meredith sang.

"The other day," everyone sang back.

"There was some snow."

"There was some snow."

"Out in the night."

"Out in the night."

"Where we can't go," Lindsay added.

"Where we can't go."

"The other day there was some snow, out in the night where we can't go," everyone sang together.

"Ms. B said to me," sang Meredith.

"Ms. B said to me."

"They lost a plane."

"They lost a plane."

"And that's a shame," Ming sang back.

"And that's a shame."

Meredith hesitated. "Line? Anyone?"

"This song's inane," Grace sang.

Meredith stopped and her face flushed pink. "You would pick the most negative word."

"It rhymes." Grace got up from the blankets on the floor and grabbed the fireplace poker. "And it's so fitting around you," she added. But I could see that she was upset and trying to cover it. Danny gave me a look, as if to say *what did I tell you?*

I realized that Grace had meant to join in. She had not expected the reaction from Meredith that she got. And if it had been anyone else who'd said it, we all would have laughed. Danny was right. Grace was trying, but it wasn't working.

"Danny!" I whispered.

The thing in the back of my mind that had been nagging at me had suddenly become clear. Danny and I had leaned into the wind when we were walking down the road to where the big pine tree had fallen. The wind had been at our backs when we headed back to the school. That meant the wind was from the north.

"I just realized something," I said. "Remember the strange way those trees we saw were lying?"

"Like an alien had pushed them over."

"Yeah. So, what if it was the plane?"

"What plane?"

"What plane? Are you serious? The airplane that's missing with those three people on it. That we just heard about on the radio?"

"I just knew you were upset about that."

"I'm not upset."

"Yes, you are. You've been stewing about it. Don't think I haven't noticed."

"Okay, maybe it's been bothering me. But listen. Everything adds up."

"Everything? Like a few blown-over trees? That plane could be anywhere, Francie."

"Not anywhere. It has to be somewhere between the Penticton Airport and Seattle. It would have to fly over here. You remember how we always hear planes droning overhead when we're at the Sasquatch Caves? This is the flight path. Dad told me about it. If the wind is from the north, planes take off into it, then they turn and fly west above the mountains."

Danny listened like she was considering it.

I went on. "Dad said the terrain can cause an optical illusion. Sometimes pilots don't realize how high the mountains really are."

"Did your dad fly?"

"No, he was just really interested in all that. We used to drive down to the airport and watch the planes take off and land."

"That's cool. You must really miss your dad."

I looked at Danny looking at me. It wasn't like her to say things like that. It's not that she didn't care; it was just that, like me, she preferred to show it without actually saying the words.

"You think I'm making this up because of him," I said.

"It crossed my mind. I mean, I know you wish you'd gone looking for your dad, so maybe you're just . . ."

"Just what?"

"I don't know, Francie."

We were not whispering anymore, and both Ming and Jasie were watching us.

I lowered my voice again.

"Well, I know one thing. If he was here right now, he'd agree with me. What if the pilot was trying to land? They missed the road, which would have been a logical place to land. The big pine was lying west to east across the road. Even though the wind was from the north. It doesn't make sense."

"Maybe the wind changed."

"It didn't. And you know it. The other trees, the ones that looked like they'd been pushed down, they were also lying west to east. Maybe it wasn't the wind that knocked them over.

Maybe the pilot was trying to land the plane on the road but got caught up in the trees."

"I know what you're going to say," she said.

"Well if you know, then why aren't you listening to me?"

"I am listening. I just think you're letting your imagination get carried away. Just stop thinking about it. Even if they did crash near here, which I doubt, there's nothing we can do about it."

"I can't believe you would say that. You of all people."

"Francie, look. I like adventures, but I have to be smart about what I do out here. If we go out and get lost in a snowstorm, I can forget about Uncle Charlie ever hiring me as a guide."

I was quiet, watching the fire crackle and spit. I felt like I was sulking, and I didn't want to sulk. She was probably right. No. She was absolutely right. There was nothing we could do. We had to stay inside where it was safe and warm while three people could be out in the worst snowstorm of the year, fighting to stay alive. It was what I'd done that night in the woods in Oregon. I'd found Dad's toque. I knew he could be nearby, but I was afraid. That's all there was to it. I was afraid, and I'd holed up and plugged my ears.

"Stop thinking about it," Danny said again. "Are you going to finish that pie?"

"You can have it."

"Cheer up," Danny whispered, shoveling up a big forkful. "You know what my grandma used to say?"

"What?"

"Don't borrow trouble."

"What does that mean?"

"Basically, you're just dreaming this up. You're imagining trouble that hasn't happened. It's not your problem."

"Okay."

"Okay?"

"Yes. Okay, okay. You're right."

"Music to my ears, as my grandma would say."

But telling yourself to stop thinking about something is harder than it sounds. I lay down and pulled up my sleeping bag, while Meredith and the others launched into their own version of "The Ants Go Marching One by One."

Ms. B got up from her knitting with a heavy sigh and went around the room blowing out the candles.

"I'll just be right here," she said, settling down on the couch, "if anyone needs me. I'll try my best not to snore."

"Ms. B!" Meredith groaned.

"Good night, girls."

"Good night, Ms. B!" everyone sang.

I watched the firelight dancing on the wall and tried to appreciate how lucky I was. A warm sleeping bag, a good fire, a building that had stood against wind and storms for eighty years. There was nothing to worry about.

I don't know about yours, but my mind doesn't work that way.

The more I tell my mind not to think about something, the more it wants to go there. It's like being told I'm not allowed in the second-floor rooms of the old wing. Suddenly, they're way more interesting than any other rooms I can go in any time.

First, my mind went to the plane soaring above the trees, looking for a place to land. Then I was at Grandpa's house, watching him dip his used teabag into his teacup as he sat at the kitchen table staring out the window at the overgrown garden. The garden had once been Grandpa's pride and joy. Once, he had scarlet runner beans climbing eight-foot poles and covered with red flowers that the hummingbirds liked. He grew pumpkins the size of beach balls and tomatoes as big as grapefruits. Hollyhocks grew against the fence and Phoebe and I made dolls from them with toothpicks, the flowers becoming pink and yellow and red skirts. But not anymore. The garden had grown parched and dusty, with weeds his only crop. It would look dead now, in late November, probably half-buried in snow tonight.

Then I was in the cockpit of the plane with snow flying at the windshield and I felt the fingers of someone's hand dig into my arm. Thinking about the pilot trying to guide the plane higher made sweat spring up on my skin, right there in front of our cozy fire. I could feel the plane tip and struggle to climb. And then I was on the ground, scrambling out of the plane.

Where was I?

Thick forest and biting cold wind. Dad's yellow rain jacket, bright against the browns and grays of the Oregon forest in spring. Half snow, half rain. He fishes his GPS from his pocket and studies it again, the thin line that is supposed to be the road up ahead.

CHAPTER EIGHT

A few weeks earlier, back in October, we had all been out in the woods practicing dead reckoning, which is a way to estimate your location based on your starting point and speed of travel. In the warm sun, a spicy aroma of leaves and pine needles filled the air, along with the whistling of hawks and the laughter of girls moving through the trees.

I realized at that moment that I was happy. For once, no sick feeling chewed at my stomach. I was glad I'd come to Green Mountain Academy. Although I'd told Aunt Sissy that I wanted to be there, I hadn't really been sure at all. I just knew that I couldn't stay in Penticton trying to live the life I'd had before. But that day in the sun-soaked woods, air soft like a warm bath, I knew I'd made the right decision.

A crackle came over the two-way radio that the sisters sometimes used when one of them took a group of us out.

"Lill, it's Lucy."

Lill unclipped the radio from her hip. "Go ahead, Lucy," she answered.

"We have a visitor. Over."

"Copy that. Who is it?"

"It's Francie's aunt. Can you bring her back to the lodge? Over."

"Copy that. We're on our way."

Suddenly my stomach clenched and the soft happiness I'd felt disappeared. Why would Aunt Sissy have come to the school? Why wouldn't she have sent an email if she had something to say? Something had happened. I knew it. And I guessed it had to do with either Mom or Dad.

Lill left Grace in charge and we hiked back, quickly covering the ground we'd taken out slowly in the morning. Lill was not the chatty type, but she looked at me sideways once and said, "Don't go getting all caught up in conjecture. You'll know soon enough why she's here."

Which, if it was meant to make me feel better, failed.

Aunt Sissy, when I saw her, didn't help any either. I could tell she had something to say by the way she hugged me— tightly, but almost in a hurry—and asked me how I was and how I liked the school, without really listening to the answers. I had to wait until Lucy brought tea and cookies to where we sat in the sunroom watching finches at the bird feeder in the yard.

Once Lucy had left us, Aunt Sissy took a sip of her tea and then pulled a brown envelope from her purse.

"They found something they think is your dad's," she said. "It's a GPS. A hunter found it."

I held my breath.

"The sheriff wants you to have a look. See if you recognize it."

She slid a photograph from the envelope and passed it to me.

I knew right away. It wasn't just the kind of GPS, with its eight small buttons in a half circle around a bigger round button. It was the lanyard that Dad had attached to it so he could loop it around his neck when he walked. The lanyard was dirty, but I could tell it was the blue one that Mom had brought home from my old school. The letters *KVR MS* that stood for Kettle Valley Railway Middle School were still visible.

There was no doubt.

"It's his," I said.

"You're sure?"

"I'm positive."

"Well, that's what I thought you'd say," said Aunt Sissy, taking another sip of tea, a frown creasing her forehead.

"Where did they find it?"

"The sheriff said to tell you it was not too far from the creek where you found his toque. As I said, a hunter came across it a few days ago. They've searched the area again, but they haven't found anything else."

"So it was just on the ground? How did it get broken?" One corner of the GPS looked as if it had been crushed. The clear plastic front was cracked. The screen had water under it and the lanyard was gray with mud.

"He said the clasp to the lanyard was broken," Aunt Sissy said. "He thinks he probably dropped it when he was walking."

"Which side of the creek was it on, north or south?"

"I don't know. I'm sorry. I didn't ask him that."

"I wonder if it still works."

"I didn't ask him that either. These are all good questions, Francie. I'll be calling him. I'll ask him all your questions."

It was a clue. Good or bad? I wasn't sure. Probably not good. He could have dropped the GPS by accident or he could have thrown it away because it didn't work. Neither of those were good. Was there any way it could be good?

Piece of crap. That's what Dad said when something he'd bought broke too soon, like the rope of mini-lights on a string that he'd wrapped around the railing of our front step at Christmas that worked for half an hour and then never worked again. Piece of crap. It was from a Neil Young song he liked. The chorus was pretty much those three words.

I could picture Dad walking through the woods with the GPS in his hand. The screen's gone blank again, like it did at home the first couple times he used it. He gives it a shake.

"Piece of crap," he says, then tosses it into the mud.

Maybe. But probably not. Dad wouldn't throw something into the trees, even if it was junk.

He had dropped it by accident, just like the sheriff said. That was more likely.

Aunt Sissy was watching me. I had become used to people watching me, waiting to see if I'd crack. Like Mom had cracked.

"I know this is upsetting," she said. "That's why I drove out to tell you."

It was upsetting, but what I didn't tell Aunt Sissy was that it was less upsetting than not hearing anything at all.

I had watched Aunt Sissy drive away. I had gone back out to the woods to try and recapture that warm feeling I'd felt. All the questions I had about Dad's disappearance had come crowding into my mind again, settling there like a dark cloud. Jasie had hugged me with her thin little arms and no words. She didn't even know what had happened, but she could read it in my face.

That night just as darkness was falling, a car engine in the school yard had startled us. No one traveled way out here on those rough roads at night. I was startled to see, in the square of light at the doorway, Aunt Sissy standing there. At first I'd imagined she'd had car trouble, something like that, some reason she'd had to turn around.

I had rushed to the door. Her face was ashen and gray under the hall light. I knew instantly. One question had finally been answered.

After Aunt Sissy left the school that afternoon, she had been almost down the hill taking her back to town when she'd picked up a cell phone signal and a message from the sheriff. When she called him back, he was having supper.

As I had imagined, Dad had not set up the tent. He'd unpacked it and draped it over his shoulders, and he'd sat under a tree, probably to wait for the rain to stop. He had not woken up, the sheriff told Aunt Sissy. Exposure, they called it.

I don't know why the detail about him having supper stuck in my mind or why Aunt Sissy told it to me. I could picture him at the kitchen table with his family around him, a jug of milk in the middle of the table, plates and forks and knives all orderly and ordinary. I could picture a TV on in the background, a jumble of running shoes on the mat at the front door. The normal things that made up a normal life I would never have again.

CHAPTER NINE

Ms. B rolled over on the couch with a groan and in a minute, she was snoring. The singing had stopped; a couple of giggles bubbled up from the sleeping bags in front of the fire. The rustlings and coughs in the room quieted and, one by one, the girls' breathing slowed into the soft ins and outs of sleep.

"Are you asleep?" I whispered to Danny.

"Almost," she answered.

"I had another thought."

"Hmm," she mumbled.

"That noise we heard when we were out hiking."

"Hmm."

"Do you remember?"

"Hmm."

"We heard a weird roaring noise overhead. You said it might be a plane. What if it was *the* plane? What if they were lost? Maybe it flew right over the school."

A log shifted in the fireplace and an ember popped.

"They can't close the school," Danny said, her voice drowsy. In a minute, she was asleep.

I tried to sleep myself, but every time I felt myself drifting, I saw Dad alone in the woods, huddling at the base of a tree, trying to stay out of the freezing rain. And then I couldn't help thinking about the plane again. I had a gut feeling, so strong I couldn't shake it. They were out there, and someone needed to help them.

I waited a few more minutes to be sure everyone was asleep, then I got up. I would need a few things.

The fire threw enough light that I could make my way out of the great room and into the hall. I found my way blindly along it to our room, then clicked on my flashlight. My knapsack was in the closet. I pulled it out and threw it on the bed.

Matches, a couple of pine cones dipped in wax that we'd made for firestarters, my compass, my knife—what else? Might as well take the little one-burner stove, canister of fuel, and the pot and plastic cups that fit inside it. Nothing like a warm cup of tea when you're all alone in the woods. An extra sweater, the old wool one that used to be Mom's. I bent and dragged the box out from under my bed. I took out Dad's Canada Post toque and snugged it around my ears.

I would have to sneak through the kitchen to get out the back door. I padded in my socks back down the hall in the dark, this time with the knapsack on my shoulder. I paused and looked at the sleeping girls in the firelight. Jasie whimpered and stirred, but then settled again. I took a deep breath and hurried through. In the kitchen, a nightlight with a backup battery cast enough light for me to find the teabags in the jar on the counter. Another jar held squares of dark chocolate. I took out two and put them in a bag with the teabags. A couple of handfuls of trail mix went in another bag. That was it. I was ready.

Then I remembered I'd left my jacket and boots by the front door. Leaving my pack on the kitchen floor, I crept back through the great room. As I tiptoed past Ms. B, she opened her eyes and brought her head up.

"Where are you going?" she said.

"I'm just getting a glass of water," I whispered.

She blinked at me a moment. Then she lay back down, dead asleep.

I was fully dressed and going the wrong way to be getting water, but luckily she hadn't noticed.

Back in the kitchen, I slipped on my jacket and zipped it up. I wound my scarf around my neck, halfway covering my face, stepped into my boots and shouldered my pack.

This was a crazy idea.

I opened the back door, felt the bite of wind and sting of snow on my forehead. I blinked against the cold air and stepped out into it.

Where was the clothesline? Where was the shed? A long drift of snow had been carved like a mountain range diagonally across the yard. Wind skimmed whirlwinds of snow off its peak. Where were the trees? Where was the fire tower on the hill? Nothing looked right.

I hesitated. Yes, maybe this was a crazy idea. I could go back inside to the warmth of my sleeping bag by the fire. I could wait until morning and set out with the others. Or we could wait for the searchers. What made me think searchers would be coming here anyway? I turned to the house. Danny was right. That plane could be anywhere. But I couldn't make myself take a step toward the door. I took a deep breath, turned again and plunged into the snowdrift. Lifting my feet high, I drove myself forward through the snow, only guessing about where the path lay.

As each boot sunk into the soft drift and I drew it up again to take another step, I felt surer. The fierce night pulled me in. The knot I'd felt twisting around my heart as I lay by the fire was loosening. I could breathe again. I gulped the wild fresh air. This was the right thing to do. Maybe not for Danny, but for me.

A little farther and I'd reach the woods. Just as I thought that, the wind relented a little and the black bulk of the forest emerged from the swirling white curtain. I pushed my legs through the snow for a few more giant steps, then stumbled onto firmer ground in among the trees.

The trees protected me from the worst blasts of wind, but their wild swaying and tossing brought a new worry. What if one snapped? What if a tree came crashing down on top of me?

"What if," Lucy had told us, was both the friend and the enemy of those trying to survive in the wilderness. It could help you think ahead to problems you might actually have to solve. But it could also make your mind fly off into imaginary disasters that would lead to panic and bad decisions.

The woods were so thick here. A snapped tree would probably not fall far before it would be caught up in the branches of another. I got my flashlight out of my pocket and shone the beam into the woods. I wasn't on the path and there was no sign of it, just the blur of snow flying at me. Normally, we tried to stick to the paths so that we didn't step on small seedlings, mushrooms, moss, and other growing things that helped connect the trees to each other. I ducked under low branches, looking for a clearing that would show me where the path was. Then I stopped. A deep roar like a rushing river traveled across the treetops. Down lower, creaks and snaps, eddies of spinning snow and bare branches shuddering in the wind.

Around me, the woods moaned and whispered. The trees had voices that changed with the seasons. In summer, the trembling aspens pattered and fluttered, each shimmering leaf snapping like a tiny flag in the breeze. The tall pines sighed and creaked as their tops swayed and their branches tossed.

What we learned from a guest that my previous teacher, Ms. Fineday, had brought out to the school in September was the real conversation between trees went on below the ground. The guest's name was Suzanne Simard and she was a tree researcher at the University of British Columbia in Vancouver. She explained that forests aren't just a bunch of trees growing randomly side by side. They're actually connected underground by a network sending messages back and forth, something like the internet. Trees talk to each other; they help each other out. When one tree is in shade, another sends extra carbon and other nutrients so it can continue to grow. Dr. Simard showed us how one tree can be a "mother tree" connected to hundreds of other trees around it. If you damage one tree, you hurt all the trees near it, too. She said it's like the rivets that hold an airplane together. You can take out one or two, but if you take out the wrong one—or too many—the whole thing falls apart.

When Lucy talked about the trees, tears sprang up in her eyes and she had to stop talking. She'd known these trees since she was a little girl. Meredith had explained that to build the kind of development that Larry was considering, they would need to cut down the whole section of forest that I was now in. Add to that the helicopters, the pollution from vehicles coming in and out, the foot traffic through the woods . . . It would destroy everything that made this place so special.

Lill was more the type to get angry than to get teary. But both sisters, when they told their first-day stories back in September, had choked up when they said that they'd made a promise to their mother before she died. They would not sell the lodge or allow any trees to be cut. They would be good caretakers of the place, and especially of the forest.

I knew the path I was looking for was on my right, probably only twenty or thirty feet away. But it wouldn't be smart to keep stumbling through the bush trying to find it. I needed to go back to where the yard ended and walk along the edge of the woods until I found the opening. Pulling my hat lower over my forehead and tightening the straps of my pack, I turned and started back through the undergrowth. Then I hesitated.

I should just go home. I looked up through the trees as snowflakes landed on my cheeks and eyelashes. The night felt like an angry friend, familiar, but still scary. I realized I had just called the school "home." It felt good. Home now was with Danny and Ming, Jasie and Meredith, Carmen and Lindsay and Grace, with the sisters and Lilac the cat.

I could smell the woodsmoke carried on the wind. The pull to go back was almost overwhelming. I took a step. Crisscrossing black branches blocked my path. Snow pelted my jacket and face, and the wind hissed through the trees like a cornered cat.

I looked for my boot tracks and followed them carefully. In a few minutes I was back to the driving wind in the open bowl of the yard. The back door beckoned. But I couldn't give up so soon. I had to at least see if there was anything to my gut feeling.

I followed the edge of the forest to the composter, and past that to the gap where the trail began. The challenge now would be to stay on the trail. My plan was to start at the place where Danny and I had heard the buzzing noise overhead. Other than the broken trees on the road, that was my only clue, the only thing that made me feel sure the plane must have landed nearby.

I couldn't hurry. In this storm, it would be easy to mistake a gap in the trees for the trail. I couldn't see the fire tower, but I knew it was just to the east of me, on a hill that overlooked the forest for miles around. If the sky had been clear, that would have been the perfect place to look for a sign of the plane. But with almost zero visibility, it wouldn't do me any good, even though the safety of the solid tower called to me.

Danny and I had spent hours in there, working out a signal system from the top of the tower to the woods. It had taken a lot of adjustment and running back and forth to find a place where one of us on the Secret Trail to the caves could pick up the signal from the tower. We'd even built a little platform in the woods that we used to boost ourselves into the bent pine tree. Then we slung a rope over a sturdy branch and tied knots in it so we could hoist ourselves higher.

From that branch, we could send signals back and forth with our flashlights. Two quick flashes with a long pause in between meant "come back to the tower." A continuous series of two quick flashes together meant "I'll meet you at the pine tree." A single flash with a long pause in between each meant "someone's coming." And of course we could use the SOS signal: three short flashes, then three long, then three short again. If someone sent that one, the other person had to get help. To let them know the SOS had been received, we replied with three long flashes. But we hadn't had to use that yet.

We'd even spent a night in the fire tower, lugging air mattresses and sleeping bags up the series of ladders to the top, along with our flashlights and snacks. In the middle of the night, I'd woken up at the sound of a clear sharp voice howling a long lonely cry out over the hills. Silver moonlight striped our sleeping bags, shining through the wooden slats of the tower.

"I'm not afraid, are you?" Danny had whispered.

"You're awake," I whispered back. Normally, Danny could sleep through anything.

"It's a coyote, I'm pretty sure," she said. "Sasquatches have a different sound. Almost human."

"Do you believe in sasquatches?"

"People have seen them."

"Have you seen one?"

"No. But I've never seen a tiger either," she whispered.

"There are tigers in zoos."

"You'd never find a sasquatch in a zoo."

We were quiet as we listened. The howl wavered and rose, as if the sound was flying across the night sky. All the hairs on the back of my neck tingled.

"I think the fact we don't know if they're real is kind of the point," Danny whispered. "It's good to be a little bit afraid. Don't you think?"

"I sort of get that," I whispered back.

"It makes you careful," Danny said.

"Why are we whispering?"

We started to laugh. The sound of our laughter rang out in the night, out into the forest, and the howling came back to us in a frenzy of yips and shrieks. That made us laugh even harder and I felt how lucky we were to be out there, sleeping in a tower among the wild things.

That's what I loved about Green Mountain Academy. What other school would let two thirteen-year-old girls spend a night alone in a fifty-year-old tower, thirty or forty feet off the ground? In fact, most schools would have fenced the tower off and posted No Trespassing signs. Have you ever noticed that most adults' immediate response to a cool idea is no? The cooler the idea, the quicker they are to say no. Lucy and Lill aren't like that. When we'd asked Lill if we could sleep overnight in the tower, she had said, "Well, I can't think of a good reason why you couldn't do that. Let me check with Lucy."

Lucy was the sister I liked the best. Most of the time she wore her shoulder-length brown hair in two pigtails that stuck out a bit from the sides of her head, and she had a favorite orange wool cap she wore no matter what the weather. She wasn't talkative. I always had the feeling she was a little afraid to talk, like she thought at any minute someone might tell her she was wrong. When her brother was visiting, I heard him say, "Lucy the dreamer. Whoever thought you'd become a teacher? I can't quite picture it. Don't the students scare you?"

And Lucy had said softly, "They don't scare me at all. Maybe children are a bit more accepting than most adults."

Lucy had a kind voice and when she spoke, we listened, because she didn't speak unless it mattered. She would often stop a sentence halfway through as she searched for the right word, saying something like, "The character in the book is not exactly . . ." And then sometimes one of the girls would supply the word: "Reliable?" And she'd say, "Yes, reliable, exactly. That's the perfect word."

Anyway, once we had Lill's approval, we knew that Lucy would agree to our idea to sleep in the tower. She told us once that the idea for Green Mountain Academy came to her because it was the kind of school she wished she could have gone to. Thinking about that made me remember the email I'd seen. I couldn't imagine leaving here now. The place I'd only just recognized as home. I couldn't believe it would happen.

As the trail curved, a gust of wind swept into my face. The bent pine that marked the start of Secret Trail was up ahead. Should I stay on the main trail that would eventually come out in the open meadow, and then follow Smoky Creek back to the school? But if I did that, I would not be sticking to my plan to return to the spot where we'd heard the engine noise.

My forehead had gone numb with cold like it did when I ate ice cream. I brought my hood up and tried to cinch it around my face. The night had grown colder. My hands and feet were warm from walking, but if I stopped for long, the cold would start to seep in. Another mighty gust. Hurtling and tumbling along in front of it was a piece of plastic or metal about the size of a shovel. I thought it *was* a shovel. It skittered along the path and slammed into a tree where it was caught, shuddering against it.

I went closer and shone my light on it. Maybe a piece of an appliance of some kind. People sometimes dumped their old appliances and trash in the bush off the road to the school. Lill had showed us a junk pile on a slope that came down off the road, near the creek.

"I don't get it," she'd said. "Who goes out for a drive and thinks, 'Here's a beautiful natural spot where I can dump my old fridge'?"

Maybe this was part of a vacuum cleaner, I thought as I looked at the metal piece again. I tapped my gloved hand on it. Definitely metal. Painted white, crumpled, but not rusted.

I stood up. I was stalling. Giant pines stirred and twisted in the wind, and a strange low whistle vibrated through the forest. Secret Trail would take me deeper into the woods, the trees thicker and the path barely a path at all. That was the whole point. Danny and I had not marked it because we wanted it to stay a secret. As easy-going as the sisters were, there were still rules at Green Mountain, and one of them was that we stay inside the area encircled by Fire Tower and Smoky Creek Trails. My chances of getting lost were stronger on Secret Trail. And then there was the cliff that dropped off to the Sasquatch Caves. I'd have to watch carefully for it so I didn't step off the edge. I fiddled with my hood a bit longer as I studied the piece of metal junk. Then I made my decision and charged forward against the wind.

My head down to protect my face from the icy air, I marched along, making good progress. Wind tore across the open meadow that lay ahead. That was when I realized my mistake. I'd got turned around the wrong way at the bent pine and come halfway along the Smoky Creek Trail. On the meadow, wind chased dry brush like tumbleweeds along the surface of the snow. I could keep going. I could be back at the school in twenty minutes if I hurried, and I could tell myself that I'd tried, at least. Really, I had no idea how to look for a missing airplane. I was just hoping. Pretending. I had no clue.

Except I did have a clue. This time, I would follow it. I turned back, the wind like claws tearing at my jacket, and I retraced my steps, more carefully now. As I got closer to where the bent pine grew, that strange whistling sound caught my ears again. I ducked into the woods onto Secret Trail. There stood the pine, patches of snow pasted against its orange trunk. The platform had blown over and was toppled on its side a few feet away. The rope we'd secured to a sturdy limb whipped out like a tail, spinning in the wind.

But I was on the right track. Not far from here, Danny and I had heard the buzzing overhead. The whistling grew more insistent. I scanned the woods with my flashlight beam. There—something out of place caught high in the branches of another big pine. The wind skimmed off it, trying to shake it loose, and the whistle came from there, another piece of white metal, larger than the other, this one striped with red and navy blue. Suddenly I knew what it was. I scrambled over the deadfall that littered the forest and stood below the tree, shining my light up into it. A tire in the metal shell was spinning in the wind, creating the whistling noise. It was a piece of landing gear from an airplane.

CHAPTER TEN

My mouth went dry as I stood staring at the spinning tire. Everything seemed to grind down into slow motion. A snowflake landed on my nose and melted. A tree creaked long and lingering in the snow-pitted night. My vision sharpened, and, in spite of the veil of snow, I saw the shape of each scale on the orange bark of the big pine trunk. My heartbeat galloped along, growing stronger in my ears and fingers and feet. I felt like the tree itself—rooted in the earth.

My mind, too, had slowed. What had only been an idea had become unreally real. It really had been a plane Danny and I heard. It had flown low over the trees—too low. The wheel had got caught up and the tree limbs had torn it off. Maybe it could still land on one wheel. But probably not, especially in this wind.

Most smaller planes had fixed landing gear, unlike the jets that only dropped it to land. I learned this from watching the aircraft at the Penticton Airport with Dad. When we drove to the south end of town to watch the landings and takeoffs, we sat in the truck and watched the small planes, helicopters and jets fly in over the valley, bucking the strong winds that funneled north and south. We had watched many small planes struggle to keep their wings level as they dropped in altitude over the runway.

Now an awareness of the cold seeped back into my mind. I stomped my feet to get the blood flowing and clapped my hands together. Then I picked my way back over the criss-crossing deadfall to Secret Trail. I had to find out what had happened to the airplane.

Only a couple hundred feet along the path lay another piece of metal about the size of a lawn chair. It was torn along one side, as if by a giant can opener. Some black substance streaked the white paint in long lines.

The cliff wasn't far now. That's where our path ended. The boulders below the cliff would be slippery with snow. I might be able to get across them, but it would be even more danger-ous than usual in the dark. And I didn't know what the terrain was like on the other side of them. I'd be marching into an unknown wilderness in the middle of the night, in the middle of the worst snowstorm of the year. To go anywhere else, east or west, would mean leaving the path.

The debris from the plane had fallen more or less in a north–south line. And where I was now was only about a mile east of the road. They could have been trying to line up with it. If, instead of backtracking to Secret Trail, I had kept going on Smoky Creek Trail, then left the trail to cross the creek, I'd eventually have ended up at an embankment I could have climbed up to the road. The plane could have landed there.

Walking more slowly now, I watched for the gap that would signal the cliff edge. I tried the flashlight again, swept it in a broad circle around me. Something glinted in the beam of light. A pair of yellow eyes blinked calmly at me from the broken limb of a dead tree. A great horned owl turned its head away and then back to me, watching with what seemed like patience to see what I would do. Well, what would I do?

His soft feathers fluttered in the wind. He wasn't afraid of me and I felt the same about him. In fact, I was glad to have some company on this crazy, lonely night. But I wished Danny were here. It always helped to talk ideas out with her—whether to turn back and head for the road, or keep going down to the Sasquatch Caves.

In spite of the cold, I'd begun to sweat under my jacket and sweater, and I knew it was fear. I recognized the tingling, heart-racing feeling, like I had a steadily inflating balloon in my chest that was on the verge of bursting. The owl called out his series of *whoo*s, twice, a gentle warning as I walked on. Then the balloon did burst.

Looming in front of me, right where the cliff edge began, one wing of the airplane was wedged upright, leaning like a slide between two trees. The red and blue stripes stood out distinctly on the top edge. At the same moment, an overwhelming smell of fuel met my nostrils.

A rush of wings beat the air overhead, and the owl's body, like a cat with wings, soared out of the blur of falling snow. Then I was on the ground.

I couldn't have lay there long. I sat up slowly. My flashlight had rolled away, still lit, shining a puddle of yellow light into the snow. The storm still swirled around me, but I felt as if a heavy calm had settled like a thick fog over the forest and the jutting white airplane wing, so out of place between the tall gray trunks and feathery cedar fronds.

I stood and brushed the snow from my pants. My pack had slipped from my shoulders and I hitched it back on, pulling the straps tight. Then I picked up the flashlight and shone it in the direction of the cliff edge.

My feet moved like I was slogging through deep mud. A sharp oily smell like the lamp oil Grandma used at the cabin filled the air. Down below the boulders, the curtain of snow parted and closed, parted and closed, on a scene I never could have imagined. The plane, what was left of it, had snapped in half over a broken tree. One half, the tail, lay across the boulders; the other, the nose, facedown in some young cedars.

I climbed down the rocks carefully. Strewn across the ground were suitcases, two of them burst open with clothes spilling out and dusted with snow. Two others were still closed. A few feet from them, a black hard-shelled guitar case, still in one piece as far as I could tell. At my feet lay a man's wristwatch with a silver strap. I picked it up. Its face was broken and I dropped it again, a chill scurrying up my spine.

I wanted to run, but I couldn't run. My heartbeat roared in my ears and I stood rooted, blinking in the dark. Slowly, that noise began to settle and I strained to hear other sounds— voices, movement, anything. Snow tapped the metal of the plane, wind swished, trees creaked. Nothing more.

I had to go closer to the wreck. I had to see if anyone was alive in there. An odor of fresh crushed cedar met my nostrils as I edged closer to the wreckage. Fuel smell again. The plane hung upside down over the broken tree. One side had been ripped open, and as I approached, I could see, through the tangle of branches, the place where the passenger seats should be. One was still there, but the other was gone. The tension in my jaw tightened. To see the pilot and co-pilot's seats, which were covered with cedar branches, I'd have to get closer.

I climbed onto a rock and parted the branches, then I shone my flashlight inside. The first thing I saw was denim. A stitched seam. I followed the stitching and saw a man's hand, a wedding ring on one finger.

"Hello!" I called. "Are you all right?"

No answer. No movement. But I knew the answer.

I reached in and found his wrist, cool to the touch. There was no pulse.

"Are you all right?" I called again. "I'm here. I can help you."

But it was quiet. I knew what it meant. The pilot was dead. It didn't feel real. I felt strangely numb.

"The pilot is dead," I said out loud. Where was the shock, the tears? I didn't feel anything. It was just a fact I had to deal with. There was no way to see any more of the man, because the wreckage blocked my view. But I could see that where a seat would have been, beside him, there was no seat anymore. Where had it gone? Where were the two other passengers? The radio report had said there were three people on board. There must be more wreckage somewhere, and if I could find it, maybe I'd find the other passengers.

In spite of the raging storm, the scene around me felt eerily still. I knew if I was going to find anyone, it had better be soon.

But still I stood there, listening, waiting for something to happen. I should have tried harder to convince Danny to come with me. Why hadn't I? Just because she hurt my feelings. Danny was the only person who never thought my ideas were crazy. But this time I hadn't convinced her. It didn't make sense. It wasn't like her.

I thought of all the sleeping girls in front of the fire. I'd broken pretty much every rule in the book coming out here. No one knew where I was. Should I go back? But since I'd come this far, there was no point turning back. If I did that, the passengers would probably be dead by the time anyone could get back to them. If they weren't already.

Reluctantly, I beamed my flashlight around the area, half afraid of what I might see. As I did, I strained my ears for any sound. And then I did think I could hear something—a low singsong sound below the roar of the wind. As sure as I was that I'd heard something, the next moment I was just as sure there was nothing. I felt like I was in a dream, not quite certain what was real anymore: an airplane in a cedar tree, a guitar case in the snow, the haunting voices of wind whispering around rocks, scolding from branches, whistling from the cliff.

And then, there it was again—two notes, and I was sure this time that it was not the wind or my imagination. But was it human? Animal? It sounded like—it sounded like what it could not possibly be. I stomped my feet to get my blood moving and shook my head clear. It was not Mom calling my name. Mom lay in a hospital bed in Vancouver, four hundred kilometers away. She had been there for months—six months, eleven days to be exact.

The call came again, and this time I recognized it as human. Someone was calling out. A surge of adrenaline mobilized me.

"I hear you!" I shouted. "Where are you?"

The rocks were slippery as I scrambled over them in what I thought was the direction of the voice. The flashlight was not really helping. When I shone it in front of me, the wind drove the snow into a spinning galaxy of flakes that almost blinded me. But whoever was out there would see the light and come toward it. That's what mattered. I struggled to avoid tripping. One of my feet crammed into a crack between rocks and my ankle twisted and sent me sideways. My right hand flew out and braced my fall against the slippery rocks. Somehow I managed to keep a grip on the flashlight in my left hand. I sat on the cold rocks.

"Well, that was stupid," I said out loud. My ankle burned from the twist and my foot was still wedged in the crevice. I wriggled it back and forth, but it wouldn't come out.

"Fran—cie!" the voice came on the wind.

No. It wasn't that. There was no one out here who knew my name. I felt tears welling up as I fought to free my foot.

I threw the beam of light out into the night.

"I'm here!" I called back.

Then I realized what I needed to do. I took off my gloves and pried at the laces of my left boot. Ice and snow encrusted them and it was hard to work them loose. Also, as soon as I'd stopped moving, I felt the cold creep deeper into my bones. My fingers moved stiffly, clumsily, but finally I managed to untie my boot. My foot was in an awkward position and I had to half-stand. Then I pulled my foot free of the boot. Now the challenge was to keep it out of the snow. If my feet got wet, there was a real danger of hypothermia. I had to put the flashlight down.

Leaving it turned on, I laid it on a flattish part of a rock. Then I pulled my left leg close against my right and bent down in a one-legged runner's lunge, both hands on the rocks to brace myself. Balancing carefully, I moved one hand to pull on the boot. It wouldn't budge. I tucked my foot under my hips, and kneeling, pushed against the rock while tugging on the boot. But it was really stuck. No amount of wrenching and shaking could dislodge it. What would I do if I really couldn't get it out? I couldn't walk through the snowy forest with one boot on.

The voice had stopped.

"Hello? Hello? I'm still here. Hello!" I shouted into the whirling snow.

I sat back on the rocks and thought about my situation. I could try to find a branch to jam between the rocks and lever one loose. But how long had these rocks been here? It wasn't likely I'd be able to make them budge. I could wrap something around my foot to use as a makeshift boot. But what? I needed all the clothes I was wearing.

Where was the voice now? Had I imagined it? Maybe it had been a bird or some other animal. I'd been so sure. But sounds can play tricks on you, especially at night. Grandpa had a fridge at his house that made a knock like someone was at the door, which I never noticed in the daytime, but only in the middle of the night, when Grandpa had gone to bed and the house fell dark and quiet.

I gave another tug at the boot. Nothing. I was wasting time. This boot was not going to move. I had to try something else. Then it occurred to me that if I had heard a human, he or she could have fallen or lost sight of my light. He or she could be wandering deeper into the woods, and if I didn't do something soon, I might never find them.

I had an idea. Although the boot was twisted, I was able to get my hand far enough into it to grab hold of the insole and pull it out. Then I took out the laces. With my flashlight turned toward my foot, I held the insole against it, then took Dad's Canada Post toque off and slipped it over my foot. I wrapped the lace around my ankle twice and knotted it. Then I cinched my hood tighter and got to my feet.

This was only temporary. I had to make my way carefully back to the plane wreck. Luckily, I hadn't got far away from it yet. I picked my way along, paying attention to the pressure on my ankle. It throbbed a little, but I didn't think it was broken. Every once in a while I shone the flashlight beam out to where I'd heard the voice and called out, "Hello! I'm here!" But no answer came back.

The weird picture of the airplane in the cedar tree shocked me again with a sense of impossibility as I neared it. It wasn't real, snow sifting in the space where the passenger seat had been, the pilot upside down in the cockpit. But it was real and I couldn't change it. I could only move step by step forward from right now. I remembered something Grandma used to say: "Give up all hope of a better past." It was one of her favorite sayings. I never understood it. Funny I remembered it now.

In my better past, Danny would have been the old Danny, hearing my idea to go on a search for the missing airplane with a twinkle in her eyes. She would have added her plans. She'd have helped me get my boot unstuck and she'd have let me use her shoulder as a crutch.

I swept the light over the scene. Men's clothes spilled from the burst suitcases—jeans, some T-shirts and dress shirts. There was nothing there that I could use. The two others, one red, one black, lay on the ground undamaged, as if someone had left them to come back for later. I chose the red one. I crouched beside it.

This seemed wrong. I was about to go through someone else's suitcase, someone who'd been a victim in a plane crash, who could be dead for all I knew. The case wasn't big but it was packed to its limit and I had to put my weight on it to get the zipper open. The top sprang up when it opened. A scent of clean clothes and perfume wafted out. A hair dryer lay on top. But I only had to move that aside to find what I was hoping I'd find, tucked into one side: a pair of running shoes. I pulled them out—lime green, too big for me, but better than nothing. In one of the pockets, I found two pairs of socks. I took the toque off my foot and put both of one pair on my left foot and stuffed one of the other pair into the toe of the left shoe.

A crawly feeling crept over me. Was I putting on the shoe of a dead woman? I shoved everything back in, including the right shoe, and zipped the case closed with a shudder. I shook the snow out of my toque and put it back on. And I stuffed the boot lace into my pocket in case I found a use for it later.

This time, I'd take it more cautiously. I couldn't afford to make another mistake. Easy to say, but in a boulder-strewn wilderness in the dark, in a snowstorm, maybe I should have expected what happened next.

CHAPTER ELEVEN

Pointless, I thought. I was heading farther away from the school, farther from safety and rescue if I needed it, and I'd heard and seen no sign of any passenger for nearly twenty minutes. Yet even as snow pellets pummeled my face and clothes, and trees creaked and groaned in the wind, the beauty of the night filled me. I was glad to be alive, glad to be out here taking in gulps of fresh, cold air.

Blood coursed through my veins, muscles pumped. I was here in this universe of hidden stars and spinning planets, an animal, surviving. I stopped to look up into the dizzying sky.

And then I heard the call again, nearer this time. I called back, flashed the light three times, then crouched down and scurried crab-like over the rocks as carefully as I could. What was it we learned in first aid? We'd learned to meet a victim with a little warning: "Hi, my name is Francie. I know first aid. Can I help you?" But that would sound too weird, coming out of the blue in this wild place.

I tried it out: "Hi, my name is Francie. Can I help you?"

That sounded like a server at a restaurant.

"Can I help you?"

No, it had to be confident.

"I can help you. I know first aid."

The call came again. I could tell it was a woman's voice, and it sounded like she was calling *John-y*. Suddenly her voice was right in front of me. I stood and cast the light in a wide arc. Maybe ten feet away stood a woman in a red leather jacket, high-heeled boots and jeans, her hair an Afro halo, rimmed with frost.

"John-Lee?" she said.

"No, I'm Francie. I'm . . . I'm . . . I came looking for you. I heard about—" I took two steps forward and felt my right foot slide. It just kept going. The flashlight flew out of my hand as I tried to grab at something. My fingers met wet cold rock and then I was falling through space.

The taste of dirt was in my mouth. Around me, cold and dark. But the wind sounded far away, moaning and scrabbling at something. Or was that an animal? Where was I? I sat up. I was on the ground, that much I could tell.

My flashlight was gone, but I still had my backpack on. In fact, I'd landed on it. Lucky. The woman had been coming toward me in the snow, and then this darkness. I shrugged off my pack and dug around in the front pocket. My fingers closed around one of the pine cones dipped in wax. I pulled it out and then a packet of matches. I struck one. In the flare I saw I was in a cave. I looked up. I had fallen down a crack and into one of the Sasquatch Caves formed by the big boulders piled here.

I dropped the match just before the flame reached my fingers. My shoulder ached a bit where I assumed I'd fallen on it, but other than that it didn't seem that the fall had harmed me. As my eyes adjusted, I could see a patch that wasn't so dark—the opening. I stood up and stretched my arms toward it. It was about four feet above me, but I couldn't see how to reach it.

With another lit match, I looked for a spot to place the wax pine cone. Partway up the slick rockface was a little indent. I set the pine cone there, then touched a flame to it. It caught and whooshed to life, throwing some light around the cave. One thing I could tell right away was that there was no way I could climb back up to the crack I'd fallen through. The walls were completely vertical and slick with trickling, ice-crusted water. Also, the crevice was over my head, in the middle of the cave and not close to the walls.

Some rescuer I was. I'd wanted to save people, but I'd made every mistake in the book and now I was trapped.

"Stupid, stupid, stupid!" I shouted.

Instead of scared, I felt embarrassed. Ridiculous to be embarrassed at a time like this, but I could picture the real rescuers, trained search and rescue people, probably four or five of them at least, with their gear and their dogs coming through the woods, shining their headlamps down on me, reassuring me with soft words and little jokes.

Suddenly, a light did appear at the hole overhead and a voice said, "Franny?"

I was so startled, I couldn't answer at first.

"Franny, is that you?"

It was a soft singsong voice. There was something familiar about it.

"Yes, yes it's me. I'm here. I fell down this hole. Are you okay?"

"I've been better, to be honest. I think my arm is broken. I can see you now. You gave me a real scare. I thought you were a ghost. And then you disappeared on me."

"This whole area is full of caves made by the rocks. You have to be really careful walking and I—well, I wasn't careful enough."

"You left your flashlight for me anyway. That was nice of you!"

I laughed in spite of the situation I was in.

"How did you find me?" I asked.

"I saw a glow. Believe me, it took all the guts I had to go toward it. I didn't know *what* it was! Am I glad to see you, Franny."

I didn't correct her. I liked that she called me Franny.

"Who were you calling? Who was in the plane with you?"

"I was calling my brother, John-Lee. I don't know where he is. My seat got thrown out of the plane when we crashed and ended up right-side-up in a tree. Still in my seatbelt, if you can believe it! I'm a little sore and I'll have some nasty bruises, but I think they're mostly from trying to get down out of the tree. I fell partway. I took one pretty bad tumble back there on the rocks, too. My tailbone feels like I've been on one epic bike trip . . ."

John-Lee. Something was adding up in my mind.

"Are you—what's your name?" I called up to her.

"I'm Diamond."

"Diamond Lee?"

"Yes, Diamond Lee."

"I . . . wow! I—"

"Now this is no time to get tongue-tied, Franny. We've got a problem to solve. We've got to get you out of this hole. Then you can explain how you came to be wandering in this god-forsaken place in the middle of the night in the middle of a snowstorm."

She was right. But Diamond Lee! The other girls would be amazed. Diamond Lee's plane had crashed in the woods behind our school and I'd found her.

"'Catch Me' is our song to do indoor chores by," I shouted up to her.

She laughed a little. "You can tell me about it when we get you out of there. How are we going to do that?"

I realized what I'd said probably made little sense to her. She didn't know who or what I was talking about. And it made me sound like a kid. I needed to focus. Forget the fact that I'd come across the crashed plane of one of the biggest singers of the twenty-first century. I was supposed to be the rescuer here. I needed to act like one.

The rope Danny and I used to lower ourselves into the caves was somewhere under the snow out there, wrapped in a garbage bag. I didn't want to send Diamond off hunting for it, since even I didn't know how close we were to it. Besides, even if she did find it, which was highly unlikely, I had no idea if she knew how to tie the proper knot. No, I needed to find a safer way out.

My pine cone candle was sputtering out. I had another, but it wouldn't burn long and we'd need it to get a fire going. Also, I couldn't hold it to move around the cave.

"I need a light so I can check out this cave. There might be a way out."

"Do you have a light?"

"I'm going to need the one you're holding."

"Okay, Franny. I'm going to try to drop it down to you without breaking it. Franny?"

"Yeah?"

"Catch it!" she sang.

I watched as she put her arm through the hole as far as she could get it, up to her shoulder. Reaching up with both hands, I could almost touch it.

"Okay, I'm ready."

"You're ready?"

"Yes."

She let it go and I caught it.

"Good job," she said. "Now I'll just wait here. In the dark. And the cold. It's very cold."

"Try to keep moving," I called. "But carefully."

"Okay, Franny. I'm counting on you."

With the light I could see that the cave was only about ten feet deep. And it was narrow, like a hallway. I moved to one end of it, but it was completely closed off by another huge boulder. I made my way along the side and found where two boulders joined. There was a very small opening, only about two feet wide by maybe a foot high. It would be tight to get through it, and where would it lead to?

I clambered up the rock and shone the flashlight through the hole. On the other side was another cave, larger than this one. I could see an opening to the outside; snow sifted through it, caught in the beam of my light. For a moment I thought how beautiful it looked. To get to that exit though, I'd have to scale a fairly steep rockface. I stuck my head and shoulders farther through the hole to get a better look.

It looked doable, as Danny would say. Except near the top where the rock bulged out. I had an inkling, and then it dawned on me. This was *my* cave and my rockface—the one I had tried and failed to climb so many times.

I scrambled back down and hurried to where Diamond was waiting.

"Diamond!" I called. (I couldn't believe I was calling Diamond by her first name. Should I call her Ms. Lee?) I called her again. And again. There was no answer. I shone the light on the hole. She wasn't there.

CHAPTER TWELVE

This was not good. This was bad. In every possible way, it was bad. She had sounded suddenly tired, I thought, when she said she'd wait for me. Tired and cold. She'd said she was cold. Signs of shock, and why wouldn't she be in shock? She'd fallen out of an airplane and landed right-side-up in a tree. She'd come across a ghost-girl in the snowy forest. I'd been surprised she had seemed so calm in the first place.

I needed to get out of the cave and I needed to find her. People die of shock. I had come this far and I couldn't let her down. In my brain, I felt determined. But deep in my gut, doubt scrabbled like a mouse looking for a toehold. I had failed at this repeatedly. But I couldn't fail this time.

I called Diamond one more time. When all that came back was the whine of the wind and the shush of sifting snow, I took my pack and went back to the cramped gap in the side of the cave.

I wouldn't be able to crawl through with my pack on my back. The gap was too small. I could shove the pack through first, but what if I couldn't fit through after it? Then I'd have lost the pack on top of my other problems. But I couldn't go without it either. Carefully, I twisted my body to get my head through. I had to twist some more to get my shoulders through. This would be tricky, but for once, being eighty-five pounds soaking wet was an advantage.

I reversed back out of the hole and made my decision. Matches and knife were in my pocket. Those were the absolute essentials. I took the compass and stuck it in my pocket, too. That was it. If I lost everything else, I'd just have to manage. I shoved the pack through, holding onto it for just a few seconds as doubt rose. Then I let it go. It dropped into the dark of the cave and I heard it land.

Suddenly my legs and arms felt like jelly. I had to do this. I had to get it right the first time. I jammed the flashlight into my pocket too and zipped it closed. Then I closed my eyes and took five deep breaths in and out to calm myself. A vision of Danny's hand came into my mind, reaching down to pull me through the hole.

"Thanks, Dan," I said out loud. And I felt a little steadier.

Once again, I twisted my head and shoulders this way, then that way, and wriggled through the gap as far as my waist. There was nothing to hold onto. I had to let my body drop forward and down to drape over the boulder. That meant my head pointed down to the ground where my pack had dropped. I couldn't see how far that was, and I couldn't get my flashlight out to check.

Feet-first was an option, but I'd be even blinder that way. No, I'd just have to hang on as long as I could with my feet and hope it wasn't too far to the ground. I slithered forward a couple more inches. Again, doubt stopped me. How did I know it wasn't a ten-foot drop? How did I know I wouldn't be landing headfirst on a rock?

I should have checked that carefully with my light before I committed to this, but I'd been in a hurry. Besides, I knew that cave pretty well, I thought. It was long and loaf-shaped inside. No, I had never noticed this gap, but I knew that both ends of the cave were low. There would not be a ten-foot drop. I was almost sure of it.

I shoved my body through another inch. Stopped. My hands clung to the cold rock. Another inch and that was the point of no return. My hands scraped the rock, I tried to tuck my head, my hips tumbled forward.

My landing was surprisingly soft. I sat up and fished out my flashlight. My hands had probably been only about six inches from the ground when I fell. Lucky. But there could be no more luck saving me from my decisions. I had to know the facts and act on them. No real rescuer crosses her fingers and hopes for the best.

I carried my pack to the middle of the cave where the snow poured in like flour into a bowl. Shining the light, I listened, hoping to hear Diamond's voice calling me. There *was* a sound: a spooky, ghostlike moaning. But that was only the wind rushing and echoing through the caves. Wasn't it? I remembered what Danny had said about the sasquatch noises.

Fear, like a creek in spring flood, suddenly poured through my veins full force. I had to get out of here. I was the one who needed rescuing now. Yes, I'd ended up in this predicament because of my own bad choices, but I'd almost succeeded. I'd been right about the plane and where it would be. If only Danny would realize where I was. If only she'd wake up and notice me missing.

But Danny had a trait I knew well from sharing a room with her. She slept like a log. No. She slept like the dead. Ravens outside our window, crashing thunderstorms, even an alarm clock wouldn't budge her. Nights when I woke to the lonely cries of coyotes in the hills, I wished she'd be awake too, so that my thoughts wouldn't go again and again to Dad, in my mind still walking through the dripping rain in the Oregon woods. I would help him set up the tent and I would get a fire going with one match. I'd wrap a sleeping bag around his shivering body and bring him a steaming cup of hot chocolate, just like he'd promised to bring me that misty morning when he set out to find help. Sometimes I whispered in the dark to try and wake Danny or even spoke her name in a soft shout. But unless I actually got up and shook her by the shoulder, she wouldn't stir.

I had two difficulties, besides the obvious one of scaling a rockface I'd failed at repeatedly. I shook my head. That was a story I had to stop telling myself. I could look at it a different way—that I had learned something. I was getting better at it. And that was true. I'd almost made it last time Danny and I were here. My problem was finding another handhold on the bulge of the rock so that I could get my left leg up.

Playing the light over the rock, I studied it. The usual trickle of water over its face had frozen in a sheen of ice. Holding onto anything was going to be hard. Then I saw it. It was so simple, I couldn't believe I'd never seen it before. What I needed to do was to get both feet on the same toehold. That would allow me to get just that tiny bit higher so I could get both hands on the bulge of the rock. Then my right foot would go where my right hand had been and I'd be home free. At least in theory. It would be a big stretch.

And I still had the two difficulties I'd started to think about: my backpack and my feet. Or more precisely, the fact that I had someone else's too-big shoe on one foot and a clunky boot on the other. There was no way I could climb in either of those. Especially if I needed to get both feet on the tiny foothold. But climbing barefoot on icy rock would be painful.

The sasquatch moans grew louder and sent a shiver up my spine. That was enough for me—I sat and began untying my boot. Danny had said sasquatches could sound almost human. This moaning sounded almost human, too. The roots of my hair tingled with fear as the moaning seemed to form into a word. Where *was* it coming from? It echoed around the roof of the cave so it felt like it was everywhere, like I was surrounded.

But what if it was human? What if it was Diamond? Hastily, I retied my boot and stood. I moved toward the gap I'd just climbed through, but the sound became more distant. Slowly, I walked along the long wall of the cave, listening. Yes, it got louder as I moved to the other end, the opposite end of the "loaf," the way I'd crawled in when Danny and I had been here. The opening at this end was low to the ground and I'd have to slither on my stomach to get through to the next cave. I crouched and put my ear to the opening.

Then I heard groans, close to screams.

"Where are you?" I shouted.

The noise stopped for a minute, then a short, sharp shout came again.

"I hear you. Can you hear me?"

I beamed the flashlight into the opening.

Whoever it was, they were probably not in the next cave and they couldn't quite hear me, I thought. But I was pretty sure the cry wasn't Diamond's. If it was human, it had to be John-Lee, her brother.

What should I do? Even if I crawled through and found him, I couldn't get him out by myself. And what about Diamond? If she didn't get warmed up and into shelter, she would die.

The answer was obvious. I needed to climb out of this cave and go get help.

CHAPTER THIRTEEN

As my bare toes touched icy rock, a shock wave shot through my legs, up my spine and into my forehead. *Don't do this*, my body screamed. I'd stuffed the shoe, my boot and socks into my backpack. The pack itself was bulkier than I wanted it to be, and I tried hard to ignore the weight of it tugging my shoulders away from the rockface. I had tucked the flashlight into the zipper of my pack so that it cast a bit of light upward, where I was climbing. It didn't do much good. I should have my headlamp. But I'd left it at the school. That's what came of rushing things.

I had to do this in one try. There was no room for mistakes, no do-overs. If I took too long, my hands and feet would stiffen up in the cold and I'd lose my grip. Getting warm again in these conditions would be nearly impossible. Snow landed on my head, trickling down my collar.

Keep your body close to the rockface, I reminded myself. *Hang off your arms, use your legs to push up instead of trying to pull with your arms.* In my head, I ran through what Ming had taught us.

Time to climb.

My fingers found the first good handhold and I swung myself up, hips close to the wall.

"This is doable," I said out loud.

The next move was a little trickier. There was only one foothold and my left leg had to swing behind my right so I could keep my balance. I also had to push off with my right hand while finding the handhold for the left.

I pictured myself doing it and then I did it. I gave myself an inner fist bump and readied myself for the next move. Already my fingers and toes were stiffening. I pushed the pain to the back of my mind and thrust myself up. For one sketchy moment I felt myself teeter as my backpack shifted and knocked me off balance. But I pressed my cheek and chest against the rockface and held on till I steadied and my heartbeat calmed.

Don't rest too long, I remembered. A blast of snow slammed me full in my face and I gasped and shook it from my hair and shoulders. I was at what's called "the crux" of my climb—the hardest part on the wall—the part I'd failed at so many times before.

I mean, the part I'd tried enough times to finally figure out.

My feet felt like blocks of ice. Actually, they barely felt like anything anymore. My fingers were worse. I flexed them, then shook out each hand in turn.

Time to move. Diamond was counting on me.

With a mighty push, my right foot found the toehold. My palms clung to the cold rock like a lizard. My fingertips moved right, left, up, down, and finally found the tiniest of swells to clamp down on. My right leg muscle burned as I powered into it and brought the left leg up to meet it.

I was on the bulge. Barely. Only my toes crammed on this slight ledge held me there. No time to rest. Just do it. I brought the right foot up and into the spot where my hand had been. I could feel my foot slipping on the icy rock. At the same moment, my flashlight slipped farther into my pack, blocking almost all my light.

In the blurry darkness, my hand found the swell of rock I was looking for. I swung my other hand up to it. Then both feet slipped off the rock and only my arms held me, hanging above the emptiness.

One second, two seconds, three seconds. My toes touched the rock again and found footing.

I drew into myself for a final push; then, like a spider in a drain, I scrabbled up and out of the hole. The world came back to me in a rush, with the full force of the snowstorm and howling wind bearing down on me. My hands and feet were beyond cold. I couldn't feel them anymore.

Socks. One on one foot, two on the other. With my blocky hands, even that simple action took too much time.

Shoes next. Boot on one foot, running shoe on the other. Tying the laces was out of the question. My fingers would not be able to do that.

Gloves. I wished I had mittens; wiggling the frozen sticks that were my fingers into each hole took forever.

I stood on unsteady legs and windmilled my arms, trying to bring the blood back into them. Then I tucked the laces into my shoe and boot as well as I could.

Light. My hands were clumsy as I tried to dig my flashlight from my pocket. Clumsiness, I knew, was a sign of hypothermia.

I needed warmth, a fire. But I also needed to find Diamond and get help for her brother.

Even finding the flashlight from where it had dropped into the depths of my backpack was difficult. I brought up the one-burner stove, then the fuel canister, then my cup, and finally the flashlight. I switched it on and did a sweep of the area.

"Diamond!" I shouted.

There was no answer, but a slight movement flickered in the corner of my right eye. I turned and focused the light on that area, calling Diamond again. Then I saw it. Covered in snow and lying on the rock about twenty feet away, a mound had shifted. My light caught the red of her jacket.

"I thought you were a snowdrift," I shouted. In a way she was. The wind had piled the snow into a peaked blanket thrown over her body. A crazy relief rushed through me like warmth. Seconds later, it turned to fear. Why was she lying there? And how long had she been like that?

My cold feet moved like bricks on the ends of my legs. Clumsily, I clambered over the jumble of snow-covered rocks toward the lump that was Diamond.

When I reached her, I knelt down and brushed the snow from her head and face.

"Wake up, Diamond."

She shifted and opened her eyes.

"Wake up," I repeated. "You have to get up. You have to get warm."

"I'm warm. I'm tired," she whispered.

"No, you aren't warm. You're freezing. You have to get up now."

Her eyes closed again. I threw the flashlight beam in a wide circle, looking for a place to shelter. The caves were sheltered, I thought, but we couldn't go down there. We might never be found. It was hard to see anything through the driving snow, but the shape of two large firs loomed not too far away. Close enough to help Diamond walk to them. Maybe.

"Let's go." I took her arm to help her up.

"I'm okay here. I'm comfortable."

"No, you're not. You're not okay." I took a breath. I had to keep the panic down, keep my voice calm but firm.

"You have to trust me. We have to help John-Lee. He's in the cave, I heard him."

"John-Lee?"

"Yes. I need you to help me. We need to rescue him."

"I don't think I can. Franny, can you go get help?"

"I will. I promise. But you need to get warmed up first. Come on. You need to get up."

"Okay."

Slowly, Diamond rose, pushing with one hand on the rock and balancing with the other on my arm. As she straightened, she cried out sharply, then sucked in her breath.

"Maybe I did a bit more damage than I thought," she whispered.

Was I right to tell her to move? Injured people are supposed to stay put. But she'd already climbed down out of a tree and wandered around a rock-strewn forest. I didn't think another few feet of walking would make much difference. And she couldn't stay stretched out on a cold rock with wind piling snow over her.

Gingerly, carefully, Diamond put one foot in front of the other.

"You make a good cane, Franny," she said. "You're a strong girl."

She didn't say "for such a little thing" or "for such a skinny twig" or any of the things people usually said, which they somehow thought were okay to say about thin girls, even though they'd never say them to chubby girls. I felt a swell of pride. Diamond could lean on me. Literally.

"Wait right here." I dug in the snow under the tree for a branch, then I used it to shake the limbs above so the snow that they held gave way, landing with a whump. Then I spread the small tarp I'd brought on the ground.

"Okay." I guided her to the protected spot and helped her lower herself to the tarp.

"That's sore," Diamond said, wincing. She took a deep breath. "You said you heard John-Lee?"

"Yes, I think so." I took out my matches and the other wax pine cone. "I was in the cave looking for a way out. I heard moaning and I think someone was calling for help."

"Did he know you were there?"

"I don't think he could hear me."

"Oh, poor John-Lee. If only I hadn't lost my phone in the crash."

"It wouldn't work out here anyway," I said.

I quickly stripped some dead branches from the fir tree. There wasn't much that snow hadn't covered. I moved like someone with no fingers or toes. My teeth had begun to chatter. Not only was I cold, but the running shoe on my left foot was now wet. If I didn't get this fire going, we'd both be in trouble.

I looked at Diamond. She was beginning to slump, her eyes struggling to stay open.

"Try to keep moving your arms and feet. You have to stay awake."

"*Catch me,*" she sang in barely a whisper. "*Just because you see me run, doesn't mean you're not the one. Catch me.*"

The song helped. I remembered sweeping the kitchen floor as Grace wiped the counters, Meredith polished the hood fan over the stove, Ming scrubbed the sink and Danny stood on a stepladder to clean the bugs out of the light fixtures, all of us singing at the top of our lungs, "Catch me!"

Even Lill and Lucy sang along as they carried in boxes of supplies from their biweekly run to town and put them on the dining room table. A pot of chili simmered on the stove, its spicy aroma mixing with the clean scent of lemon dish soap. The school building with its solid wood beams glowing warmly in the bright morning sunlight felt so safe then, so perfect and protected, like nothing could touch us, nothing could change or break our circle of happiness.

But that was before I read Lucy's email. That was before her brother's threat to close the school by Christmas. I was sorry I'd read the email. It was better not to know. Wasn't it?

I struggled to light the fire. One match, two matches, three matches, each one flared briefly, then died out, leaving a small curl of smoke to twist into the wind.

"Franny." Diamond interrupted her song. I turned to her.

She sat up a little straighter and with shaky fingers, unzipped her red leather jacket.

Just then I remembered Mom's sweater I'd stuffed in my pack. As I pulled it out, Diamond pulled some rolled-up sheets of paper from her inside pocket. Her hand shook violently as she handed them to me.

"My new song," she said. "I was writing it on the plane. Guess what it's called."

I wrapped the sweater around her shoulders and took the papers from her.

"Burn Me Once!" She laughed weakly, then winced in pain. "That's what it's called. How perfect is that? *Burn me once, shame on you. Burn me twice, shame on me* . . . Start the fire with it."

"Are you sure?"

"It's perfect. Anyway, I've pretty much memorized the lyrics. And we need heat."

I crumpled Diamond's new song into three tight balls, then tucked them around the wax pine cone and teepeed twigs over that. I had some larger branches beside me to add once it got going. Meanwhile, I struggled to keep the panic down. All of this was taking too long and we needed to get to John-Lee before—well, before something even worse happened to him.

I knew Diamond was thinking the same thing. She was trying to keep me calm and focused. Her voice shaky with cold, she sang me a bit of her new song. "*There won't be a third time. I'm setting myself free. Burn me once, shame on you. Burn me twice, shame on me.*"

I lit another match and touched it to the paper. This time it caught and lit the waxed pine cone. It flared to life and the twigs ignited. As I fed it bigger branches, the welcome heat radiated out like a warm embrace.

"Amazing!" said Diamond.

"Can you move closer?"

She tried to push herself up with her hands, but she collapsed with a cry of pain.

"It's okay," she said when she saw my worried look. "I can feel the heat. Thank you, Franny."

I warmed my hands, getting as close as I could without burning myself. Then I took off my boot and the shoe and warmed my feet and socks.

"Franny? Do you have two different shoes? And is that my running shoe?"

I laughed. "It's a long story. But yes. I hope it's okay."

"Okay?" she said. "I'm honored."

When my socks began to steam and my feet were warmer, I gingerly shoved them back into the cold footwear. I fished out the squares of chocolate and snapped one off for Diamond. I put the rest away in case we needed it later.

"Eat this. It'll help. And drink this water." I took out a water bottle.

"You eat it. You need it more than me."

"No, I'm fine," I said, although I really wanted that chocolate.

Diamond took it reluctantly.

"It's frozen," she said.

"Just let it melt in your mouth. It'll help you stay awake."

I broke more branches from the tree above us and piled them near Diamond. Her head had dropped to her chest. I shook her awake.

"I'm going for help now," I said. "You have to stay awake. You have to keep the fire going so I can find you again. And find John-Lee."

"Yes, okay. I'll write more verses to my song. That's what I do when I'm on a long road trip and trying to stay awake at the wheel. I sing verses to the songs I'm writing."

"I'll be as quick as I can. Sing loud."

I pulled my hood tighter and took a step away from the warmth of the fire.

"Franny?"

"Yes?"

"I'm worried about you walking into that storm all alone. Do you know where you're going?"

"Don't worry. I'll be back soon."

As I plunged back into the storm, I realized that I hadn't really answered her question.

CHAPTER FOURTEEN

Trusty old tree.

In the swirl of snow and bite of cold, the solid trunk of the bent pine appeared like arms reaching out for me. I shuffled through the snow that had piled around it and put my hands on the rough bark. I had the strange feeling then that the world around me had disappeared and I was all on my own. Except for the bent pine.

"I'm still here," it seemed to say. Its friendliness rushed through my bones, bringing a spark of warmth. I sheltered under the tree to catch my breath.

Something had bent the pine when it was young—a hard wind, an animal? But it had not broken. It had bent and kept growing, becoming unique and strong. Tears filled my eyes, but they were not tears of fear or helplessness.

The storm would end. The morning would come. These were things I knew for sure.

After I'd left Diamond, I'd fought my way through the slashing wind, stepping carefully among the rocks so I wouldn't make the same mistake twice. Diamond's song carried on the wind, getting fainter and fainter until I couldn't be sure what was her voice and what was the song of the trees straining to stay upright in the storm.

Now, as I held onto the bent pine, I wondered how much longer I could walk in the cold. My foot in the boot still had feeling in the toes when I wiggled them, but the foot in Diamond's running shoe was numb. Maybe I could just rest for a few minutes under the shelter of the pine. I tilted my head back to see if there were branches loaded with snow that could dump on me if I lay down underneath them.

Suddenly a white streak of light blazed across a triangle of sky that I glimpsed through the branches. Lightning. Was there such a thing as lightning in a winter storm? I was pretty sure I'd heard of that. Thundersnow, it was called.

Unless I'd just imagined it. Maybe I was seeing things. I looked at my watch. Quarter to two in the morning. I'd been awake for almost twenty hours. I could be hallucinating.

I stepped out from under the branches and looked up into the snow-fuzzed sky again. But it wasn't a hallucination. A sweep of light like the Milky Way washed the sky for a few seconds and then disappeared. Then it passed over again.

I was sure then that it wasn't lightning. It was too regular. Two in the morning. Where would it be coming from? It was too far to the east to be coming from the school. East of the school was . . . the tower.

Yes!

I squealed in joy. If the wind hadn't been roaring so hard, anyone within eight kilometers probably would have heard me.

Someone was in the old fire tower, sending a signal. And that someone had to be Danny.

I shook off my pack and pulled the knocked-over platform back to the tree. Then I grabbed the rope we'd tied in it and boosted myself up onto the flattish part of the trunk. From here I could reach another sturdy limb and pull myself to standing. This was the spot Danny and I had worked out for signaling to the fire tower.

I switched on my flashlight. My hands trembled, but now it was with excitement. I flashed three short bursts of light into the storm, followed by three long and then three short again. SOS. Danny would recognize the signal we'd practiced. If she could see it through the thick-slanting snow.

That must be why she had beamed her signal into the sky like a searchlight. I climbed a bit higher to get clear of the overhanging branches. Now I had a line of sight to the open sky. I sent the SOS signal into the night and crossed the frozen fingers of both hands. A cloud of breath billowed around my face. I stomped my icy feet carefully on the tree limb, trying to warm my blood.

No response came. But it had to be Danny. There was nothing else around here for miles and miles. Should I climb down and continue on the path?

I tried again—three short bursts, three long, three short.

Then, disaster. As I tried to put my flashlight carefully in my jacket pocket, I missed the pocket altogether and the light went clattering to the ground and blinked out. But as I looked up from where it had fallen, the sign came back: three quick flashes that meant *I saw you, I'll get help.*

I was so happy I grabbed the rope and swung down to the ground in one smooth monkey-move. I sifted in the snow and found the flashlight, then picked it up and knocked it against my hand. But it was no good. The light was out. And with my fingers like frozen sausages, I couldn't try to fix it. I shoved it in my pocket and kicked myself again for not taking the time to pack my headlamp.

Now I just had to wait. I hunched against the pelting snow and wind, snugging my face into the front of my jacket. But I was freezing. There was no way I could stand here and wait. I had to keep walking, light or no light.

For a moment, I wondered if I was thinking clearly. Cold and fatigue can cause your brain to slow down like water in a stream turning to slush. Lill had taught us that during winter safety classes. I had no flashlight. I could lose the path. Danny and I had lost it coming back—was that just this afternoon? It seemed like days had passed.

I could make a fire and wait here by the bent pine. But the effort that would take seemed overwhelming. Besides, Diamond and John-Lee couldn't last much longer out there. If I could get to the school soon, I could help to organize the rescue. And that, I was pretty sure, made good sense. My mind hadn't turned to slush yet.

I took the turn for Fire Tower Trail and set out, almost at a run. The path here was well-groomed and wide. Lill and Lucy trimmed the undergrowth back in late spring. The girls helped keep it under control when we went for hikes, snipping back any new growth that had spread to the path. In October, a tree had fallen across it in one of the big storms and Lill had to bring out the chainsaw. She sawed it in two places then dragged the log to the side of the path.

Lucy said that Lill had every tool known to humankind. That was when Lill had fired up the leaf blower during our English class. Lucy had looked out the window and shaken her head. "Raking leaves used to be a peaceful activity," she said quietly in a lull from the noise.

During another English class, Lucy had looked over at the window and then done a double take. All of us turned to see Lill's legs disappearing up the rungs of a ladder, the small chainsaw hanging from one hand.

Lucy threw open the window and shouted, "Lill, what are you doing?"

"I'm trimming the branches near the roof," Lill shouted back.

"I told you before to ask for help!"

"I'm perfectly fine!"

They fought, like any sisters fought, but somehow their fights always had a bit of love in them.

But you have to fight back when someone says something mean. Don't you? Mom calls that taking the bait. I hardly ever fought with my twin sister, Phoebe. But when it mattered the most, I took the bait. My mind drifted back to that summer day at Gem Lake. I could feel myself slipping down into the memory when suddenly a fallen tree appeared, blocking my path. It was buried in snow and I'd almost walked right into it. It could have come down in this storm, but it had the look of something that had been here for a long time.

I turned and looked behind me. Another fallen tree lay in what I thought was the path I'd come down. It, too, was buried in snow. But that was impossible. That wasn't the path, obviously. But where was it? Between those two trees? Or those? And where was it in front of me? Was I even on the path? A whirlwind of snow shape-shifted around me. I was dizzy with it.

My mind had not been here in the winter storm. It had been off in the green summer woods with hummingbirds darting from tree to flower and sun shimmering on the lake. A clammy sweat prickled my skin, though I was still freezing. It was the sweat of fear. I could *not* be lost. I could not have done the same thing Danny and I had done earlier in the day. I'd been so sure of where I was going.

Nothing looked right: nearby, snow-covered tree trunks, straight, swaying, then the wild slanting flurry of pelting snow. I had to calm down. I breathed in; my exhaled breath came out ragged, choppy.

I looked up to try to find the signals from the fire tower in the sky. But branches blocked my view. Without a light, without anything to orient myself in the whiteout, I knew I was in trouble. Then, beneath the roar of wind, I heard a different sound: a faint whistle. I stood stock-still and listened. Moan of wind, squawk of trees bending.

Was there something else? It whispered then faded in the wind. The path couldn't be far, but I had no sense of which way to go. I felt paralyzed by uncertainty. Then again, the whistle. Two high, two low. Only one person I knew could whistle like that.

"Danny!" I shouted. "I'm here!" I couldn't whistle at all, but I wore a whistle around my neck and I dug it out now. My frozen lips closed around it and when I blew, the sound came out high and feeble.

"Danny!" I called again.

Then I saw the light, bobbing through the driving snow like a headlight on a lonely road. I whistled again. For a moment, a beam of light blinded me, then Danny said, "I found you! I was starting to think I was wrong. I mean, I *was* wrong. I should have listened. I knew it, I just couldn't tell you and I thought you'd just—I never thought—I mean I never told you, so—holy smokes, Francie, am I ever happy to see you!"

She clapped me on the shoulder, then we hugged and laughed, though my mouth was so frozen I sounded like a cackling witch.

"But if you're here, then who's in the fire tower?" I asked.

"You'll never believe it. It's Jasie!"

"Jasie? I saw her signal."

"She woke me up. She told me you'd been gone a long time. She'd seen you with your jacket on, and when you didn't come back to your sleeping bag, she got worried. And I just knew then."

"Danny, I found the plane."

"I knew it! Where did they land? Are they okay?"

"They crashed in a tree. The pilot's dead."

"Dead?" Danny stared at me as the storm howled around her. We'd been shouting over the noise of it and now she spoke so softly it was hard to hear her. "Oh, I'm sorry. I'm sorry I didn't listen. I—"

"We couldn't have helped him. But what do we do now?"

I explained about the crash and Diamond and her brother.

"I told Jasie if she saw the SOS signal to go for help," Danny said.

"I sent the signal. She saw it. She sent back the reply."

"Then she'll be going for help. But we have to get you to shelter. I think we should go back to the school. You can get warm and direct the rescue from there."

As we'd been standing there talking I'd been stomping my feet and getting colder and colder.

"I can't leave Diamond much longer. I could go back to her and you could go to the school."

"I'm not leaving you alone."

"I made a fire for her. But it'll burn down and—"

"Okay," Danny said, her voice firm and calm. "Here's what we'll do. Come on. You need to walk. Take me to the crash. We'll warm you up there. Grace will know what to bring—rope, good lights, blankets."

She handed me my headlamp and put her own on.

"You forgot it," she said. "I saw it with your stuff, so I grabbed it."

"Thank you."

"Wait. What are you wearing on your feet?" she said.

"A running shoe. It's a long story."

"Take my boots," she said, kneeling down to untie them.

"Your feet are bigger than mine. You won't be able to wear my boot."

She hesitated and thought for a minute. "Okay, that running shoe looks big enough. Switch that with me. You take my boot."

I grabbed her arm. "Danny, I—"

She thought I was going to argue. "No, listen. I was wrong before, but I'm right now. You're too tired to be making decisions."

"I was just going to say I'm glad you're here."

We both laughed, my cackle tight in my cold mouth. I bent and took off the snow-soaked running shoe, then slipped on her warm, dry boot. She didn't wince as she wedged her foot into the wet shoe.

❖

Danny led me back to the path. I'd only been steps away, but even a few steps in the blank, snowbound woods could have been enough to lead me hopelessly off course. Just having Danny with me had made everything seem possible again. I even felt warmer.

Danny hurried along the path at a light jog, glancing behind now and then to make sure I was keeping up. I felt the blood returning to my feet. When we got to the bent pine, we had to slow down.

"I can barely make out Secret Trail," Danny said.

We paused as I pointed out pieces of wreckage to Danny.

"Searchers would never find this now," she said. She was right. The white pieces of airplane had become almost impossible to see in the drifts of snow.

When we reached the place where the plane had finally come down and broken over the trees, it was even stranger. I scanned the area, seeing no trace of it. Danny stared too.

"Are you sure this is where you saw it?" she asked.

I didn't answer. I've read that when people are close to death, their whole life plays out like a video on fast-forward in front of their eyes. I wasn't close to death—at least I hoped I wasn't—but something like that seemed to be happening to me as I stood scanning the trees for the airplane. Was it real? Was there even a school called Green Mountain Academy? Lucy and Lill, the sisters—had I met them for the first time back in August? Had Aunt Sissy driven me into the deepening forest with clearings now and then bathed in golden light while Mom lay in St. Paul's Hospital in Vancouver?

Where was Dad? Was it really true that the last time I'd seen him he was wearing a backpack and a yellow rain jacket and hiking into the rain falling on the tall firs of the Oregon forest, leaving us behind? It didn't seem possible, Dad who walked all day in his job as a mail carrier for Canada Post and who spent every night after work sitting in a reclining chair that had the imprint of his head and elbows and legs in the soft green cushions. What had happened to my life? Was it all a dream?

Danny shook my arm gently.

"It's okay, Francie, I see it now," she said.

CHAPTER FIFTEEN

Danny's reassuring voice brought me back to the reality of snow and sharp wind. I saw then what she saw: the jagged ripped cedar tree, the blue and red stripes on the white airplane body—broken in half and being buried slowly by snow and cedar branches so deep green they looked black in the light from Danny's flashlight. The smell of fuel had disappeared and, with it, the sense that anything had just happened here. Instead, it seemed grown over, old, an accident that we were discovering years after it had happened.

"Whoa," said Danny quietly. "It's amazing anyone survived that."

"Diamond is this way. I hope the fire is still burning."

"Are you cold?"

"I'm okay," I said.

As we scrambled over the snow-covered rocks and boulders, I tried to listen for John-Lee's cry below the howling wind. He had to be in one of the caves underneath us. Somehow, like me, he must have fallen down a hole while trying to find his way. He must be scared and freezing. I just hoped we could get to him in time.

After a few minutes of careful climbing, Danny suddenly cried, "I hear something!"

We stopped and listened, Danny's hand up like she was directing traffic.

"Do you hear it?" she said. "It sounds like . . . singing."

"It's Diamond!" I shouted. I blasted my whistle three times to let her know that we were coming. Not that she'd know what it meant. It might even confuse her. "Let's hurry."

"Don't hurry, Francie. You're always telling me that. These rocks are dangerous."

"I know, I know. You're right."

"Just take it slow and steady. That's what my grandma used to say."

"Sounds like my grandma."

"Francie, there's something I have to tell you."

"Now?"

"I just want you to know. Why I didn't want to search for the plane last night."

"I thought you said I was imagining the whole thing."

"I know. But that wasn't quite true. I did think there was a chance the plane could be near here. But I didn't want to go look."

"Why?"

"That's what I'm trying to tell you," she said, a snap in her voice. "My grandma—she was fifty-nine when she died. I know that sounds old, but she wasn't that old."

I wondered where Danny was going with this. What did her grandma's age have to do with a search for a missing airplane? I took a step onto a large boulder and it shifted under my foot. Danny grabbed my arm and pulled me up before I landed.

"Careful," she said.

I was too tired to make our usual joke.

"She wasn't a typical grandmother. She hunted. She'd go out for a week with just the basics: a little pot, some tea and sugar, flour, salt, a jug of water. She'd bring her .22 and a small tarp. And shortbread cookies. She could kill a deer with a .22 in one shot. No suffering."

Danny stumbled, then fell to her knees on the rocks. I helped her up.

"Ouch," she said. "I don't want to do that again."

"Careful," I teased her.

"Anyway, I know some people think hunting is cruel. But we never waste anything. It's almost all used and what can't be used is left for the coyotes and wolves and bears," Danny said. "And it's not just for fun like some people think. Our people have always hunted and fished. But you can't just take. You have to give back, too."

"And your grandma?" I asked.

"Well, she went out one fall day like she usually did. It was five years ago. I was eight. She got caught by a snowstorm. She never came home."

"Oh Danny."

"We found her five days later. She'd broken her leg. What they figure is that she couldn't walk to find wood to make a fire and she froze to death."

I knew how Danny felt, knowing a person you love needed your help, and you weren't there to help them.

"Why didn't you tell me before?"

"I didn't want you to think I was comparing what happened to her to what happened to your dad. Grandma died doing what she loved," she said. "And I didn't want you to think I was chicken."

"I would never think you were chicken. You're the bravest person I know."

Danny made a snorting noise. She didn't like compliments and she didn't like mushy. We had that in common.

The singing was getting louder, but there was still no sign of Diamond, no sign of a fire. Danny and I crab-walked the next few feet over a bad slippery section.

"I guess I've been a bit afraid of winter storms ever since then," Danny said.

"I would be, too."

"But I shouldn't have let you go out alone."

"You didn't know. I snuck out. I did it on purpose. I didn't want you to try and stop me."

"But I should have known."

"You're here now. And we're close to Diamond. I can almost make out the lyrics."

"Is it 'Catch Me'?"

"I think it's her new one—'Burn Me Twice.'"

"Where is she?"

"I can't see the fire," I said. I swept my headlamp across the boulders and into the trees.

"Diamond!" I called. But the wind threw the name back into my face.

"She's close," said Danny.

"She should be under those trees, I think . . ."

"John-Lee?"

I swung my flashlight and there she was, huddled under the tree, with snow draped over her one exposed side. The fire was almost out. We could have walked right by her.

"Find some firewood, Francie," Danny said. "I'll get my stove going and brew up some hot chocolate. You both need to get warm."

I dropped my pack under the tree, glad to have Danny taking charge.

"John-Lee?" said Diamond again.

"I'm Danny. I'm here to help."

She set down her pack and started pulling things out as I went to gather some wood. I knew she'd asked me to do that because I needed to keep moving until the fire was going again. I also knew that Diamond's confusion was a bad sign. It meant that she was moving to the second stage of hypothermia—what search and rescuers call the "umbles"—stumbles, mumbles, fumbles and grumbles. If we didn't get her warm soon, she'd be in real danger.

As I broke dead branches from the lower limbs of the pines and stripped some twigs of orange fir needles for tinder, I tried to think logically about what we should do. First, we had to let the other girls know where we were. But what would we do next? Even if one of us hiked back to the school to ask Ms. B for help, there was no way of driving out. The road had been blocked by the fallen tree and, in the other direction, the road just petered out. There were no houses back that way.

Without cell phone service, with the power out, there was no way to get a message out. The only possibility would be for some of us to hike out on the road. But it was almost twenty kilometers to the nearest house. It would take hours. When the weather cleared and daylight came, they'd be looking for the plane, but that would be hours, too.

The only chance John-Lee and Diamond had of surviving was in our hands—the girls of Green Mountain Academy. Everything we'd been learning about in the classroom and what Lill called "scenarios" had become real. We couldn't make any mistakes. Two people's lives depended on us.

CHAPTER SIXTEEN

Fire crackled and threw dancing shadows on the fallen snow that had drifted under the tree. Squatting beside it, Danny fed more branches into the red embers. She looked mesmerized by the twisting flames, but I knew Danny enough to know she was worried. In the firelight, her forehead was wrinkled and her dark eyebrows were set in a fierce line.

Diamond and I cupped in our hands the sweet hot chocolate Danny had mixed up for us. I could feel my chilled body warming as I leaned in closer to the fire. The fir boughs, full of sap, sizzled and snapped like electricity and spit a shower of sparks that landed harmlessly in the snow.

"Take your boots off, Francie. Warm your feet," Danny said.

I did as she said and sat rubbing each icy foot as the little fire slowly brought the color back to them. Danny had stacked some bigger boughs between two trees to make a wind break. She'd laid a plastic tarp on top of other boughs so that we wouldn't have to sit on the cold ground. And she'd brought fleece blankets that she'd wrapped around Diamond and me. Danny took out cookies, peanut butter ones that Meredith had baked the day before, and passed them around.

"You girls," Diamond whispered, and she tried to smile.

"Are you feeling any better?" Danny asked her.

"Much better. But I don't think I can walk."

"You're not going anywhere for now. One of us will stay with you and the other will go back to the path to meet the other girls."

"But John-Lee," I said.

"We should wait until we have help," Danny said.

I knew she was right. My body was only too happy to wait. I could have stretched out there, pulled the fleece blanket over my shoulders and let Danny watch over the fire as I slept. I was so tired. The night would not let up.

I looked at my watch: 3:05 a.m. It was the time of night when I was stranded in the Oregon woods that I felt like I'd never see morning again, when the chill of night dug into every bone in my body and made sleep almost impossible. It was the time when I thought I couldn't go on anymore.

Even now, months later, I'd wake up in the room I shared with Danny, my mouth dry and my heart pounding and my bed spinning in the dark until I slowly recognized the gooseneck lamp beside my bed, the desk, the patchwork quilt, and the shape of Danny hunched beneath her blankets in the next bed. The ache of missing Mom and Dad sat like a big black dog on my chest, its massive paws pinning me down as I struggled to catch my breath.

Then I thought of Phoebe. I felt her hand reach down for me and pull me up from the deep dark hole I was slipping into. I clung to the memory of her and tried to breathe.

Now, with the night and the storm raging on just beyond the light of our cozy fire, I replayed the moment I spotted Dad's blue and red Canada Post hat that night in the Oregon woods. All the things I should have done then to find him marched through my mind. There was no end to things I thought of that would have been better than what I did do.

I had crawled into a shelter and saved myself. I had done the right thing, searchers told me again and again. My brain knew it to be true. But I had not convinced my heart.

"Danny," I whispered.

She looked at me across the fire. I could tell she already knew what I was going to say.

"I'm going to look for John-Lee."

Diamond had curled up by the fire with the blanket wrapped around herself. I didn't think she could hear me.

"I have an idea where he is. If he's injured, he might not last the night."

"You know you shouldn't go into those caves alone," she said.

"I'll set up the rope anchor we usually use," I said. "I can lower myself down that way."

"We could wait for Ming," she said. But I could hear in her voice that she agreed with me.

"I know my way around down there. I can always come back to the rope to get out."

"Okay," Danny said. "But I'll set up the anchor. And I need to be right there in case you get into trouble. We'll find John-Lee then I'll go out to the trail to meet the other girls. If they don't find us first."

"What about Diamond?"

Danny looked over at Diamond, who seemed to be sleeping, then back to me. I could see she was torn.

"Let's make sure she's warm before we leave her."

We leaned into the fire, each of us lost in the thoughts that couldn't be shared. Then Danny said, "If we don't find him . . . Or if . . ."

She trailed off, and I knew that each of us was not just thinking of John-Lee.

CHAPTER SEVENTEEN

It was harder to find the entrance to the cave than I expected. Snow had transformed the familiar shapes of boulders and fallen trees. So many cracks and crevices, some bottomless, hid in the rocks that we had to inch along, feeling our way as the storm tore at us and made it hard to breathe.

We finally found it by recognizing the tree we used for an anchor.

"Look! Here it is," Danny shouted. "The opening will be right there." Her light lit up the protective canvas cuff we'd fastened to the tree so we wouldn't damage it with our rope. Then Danny dug in the snow and pulled out the garbage bag with our rope in it. The rope was stiff with cold as we unraveled it.

I made my way to the opening. A depression in the snow warned me before I got too close to the edge. With a branch, I swept it clear as Danny tied the rope around the tree trunk with a bowline knot backed up by a single fisherman's. We didn't usually go down into the caves this way. Usually, we crawled through the openings and only used this as a way to get out if we needed it.

This wasn't the safest method of rappelling. But it was fast. We didn't have climbing gear or even a long enough rope to reach the bottom. I'd have to get as close to the bottom as I could, then drop. And I'd have to be careful not to bash myself against the rock wall as I did.

Earlier—it was yesterday now—I'd crawled through a series of low, dark and wet tunnels to end up at the rockface I'd been trying to climb. I was pretty sure John-Lee was somewhere in those caves; I'd heard the moaning coming from that direction. But trying to crawl through those tunnels now would waste time and what little energy I had left.

Standing beside me, Danny put her weight on the rope to test its strength. Then I tied butterfly knots in the middle of it and tossed it down the hole. The butterfly knots made stirrups that I could use for foot and handholds, but they also made the rope shorter.

I looked up at the sky. So did Danny. No sign of the storm letting up. The wind sent snow hissing across the rocks. If anything, the gusts had strengthened. Danny's hair whipped her cheeks and we both struggled to stay on our feet.

"Are you sure about this?" she shouted.

"Not really," I shouted back.

She laughed, her eyes twinkling. She knew me well enough to know that wouldn't change my mind.

"Keep an eye on Diamond," I reminded her. We looked in that direction, but it was a total whiteout. We could barely see three feet in front of us.

"That's my job," she said. "This is yours."

The first few steps were the hardest—getting over the edge. I lay on my stomach and wrapped the rope around my arms, then I let my feet dangle and find the rockface. Once they did, I leaned back with my weight on the rope. I thought of what Dad used to say: *Trust the tools.* He said that if you were careful enough to choose the right tool for the job, then you had to trust the decision you'd made. There was no point in being half-hearted about it. Trust the tools. I would try.

I moved carefully, lowering myself from loop to loop. I had my headlamp, but it didn't help me see the footholds. I had to go by feel. Danny peered over the edge, watching my progress.

When I reached the limit of the rope, I pushed off the rock with my feet and let myself drop, landing shin-deep in fluffy snow. I brushed myself off and looked around.

Everything looked different down here too now. Snow had sifted through the cracks in the rocks and left white shapes draped like cobwebs in the cave. I guided myself to the far end of the loaf-shaped cave where I'd heard the moans coming from earlier. But only the wind whistled and squawked through the gaps and crevices now. What if I was wrong? What if it hadn't been John-Lee I'd heard at all? What if it had been something else?

"Francie?" Danny's shout pulled my mind back from the scary edge it was creeping toward.

"I'm okay!" I shouted back. "Heading out to the next cave."

"What?"

I made my way back to the rope. Danny's headlamp almost blinded me.

"We need signals," Danny said. "Two quick flashes of light mean you're okay. Three mean trouble."

"But I might not be able to shine it somewhere you can see."

"Use your whistle then. Blow loud."

"Okay. I'm heading out."

I don't know if Danny could feel the hesitation that I felt.

I shifted my backpack and took a step. I had to admit it—I was scared.

"Francie!" Danny shouted again.

I turned to see her face like moonlight at the rock opening. "Be careful."

"I thought I'd—" But my mouth had gone dry and I couldn't finish the joke.

I tried not to think about the fact that I was in the middle of a snowstorm, heading into a labyrinth of boulders toward a strange low moaning sound that might or might not be human.

The opening into the next cave was easy enough to squeeze through. I'd done it many times, from the other direction. I crawled on my hands and knees then shoved myself up over a lip of rock and I was in. But without the friendly wink of sunlight through the cracks, I had that same sense of doubt that I knew this place.

My headlamp lit up snow dusting down through the openings, but the corners remained in shadow. I looked for something

I recognized——that ledge; that was where I'd imagined putting a candle if I ever had to spend the night in here——wasn't it? I should try to remember that feeling, a tingle of anticipation. The smooth rock shelf was covered by a couple inches of snow and I couldn't be sure.

"Francie?" Danny's voice came, fainter now.

"I'm okay!" I shouted back.

"Francie?"

Already she couldn't hear me. I fished out my whistle and blasted it twice.

A few seconds later I heard something else——a faint cry like a bird. Maybe an animal. What were the chances of some animal hibernating in among these rocks? Bears, for instance. Or even skunks. Cougars don't hibernate, but they like to sleep in protected places like these caves. Coyotes and wolves might even build their dens in here.

"I hear you!" came Danny's voice.

Then a squawk, almost a hiccup, soft, muffled. Was it human? I moved toward the sound. How close? My stomach churned, telling me to turn back. I stuck my head through the next opening and listened in the dark hollow space. Haunting moans swirled and echoed. The smell of mud and cold and musty corners that had never seen daylight filled my nostrils.

I forced myself forward on elbows and knees, flattening my body even more as I inched into the next cave. It was smaller than I remembered. I could barely sit up, my head touching the damp stone. I blew the whistle twice, loud, and listened.

No answering whistle. Just the angry hiss of the storm flinging itself in fits against the earth. I doubted whether I could hear anything with the storm drowning out everything. Then the squawk—faint, but distinct—echoed against the rock walls.

It was not an animal, I was sure of it now. It was human and I was getting closer.

CHAPTER EIGHTEEN

I hadn't wanted to admit it. I told myself the storm was the reason I couldn't hear Danny's answering whistle. But the cave I found myself in after squeezing through narrower and narrower openings now confirmed the doubt that had been blossoming slowly in my gut.

I was no longer in the caves I knew. I'd followed the squawk, toward what had to be John-Lee. But where I was now, I couldn't say for sure.

Three other realizations hit me, one after the other: I was cold, I was hungry and I was tired. In spite of the protection from the storm that the caves offered, wind found its way through some openings and sent drafts of icy air and snow shivering down my neck.

Water trickled from the rocks and had pooled in the cold mud. The knees of my pants were soaked and my eyes felt like they'd been scrubbed with a toothbrush. It was the middle of the night and I shouldn't be awake, let alone out in a whiteout storm, crawling underground in a labyrinth of sasquatch caves.

I took out my water and squirted out a mouthful. It helped a little. I wanted something hot—oatmeal with brown sugar and apple slices (our usual breakfast weekdays at school) or scrambled eggs and toast, our weekend breakfast. Last Saturday, Meredith made a frittata with tomato slices, mushrooms and bubbly cheese melted on it. But nothing could beat Dad's homemade hash browns that he only made at Christmas and Thanksgiving and that took him a couple of hours. Crispy and spiced with the garlic and rosemary and parsley that Mom grew in her garden on the south side of the house. The rosemary and parsley both survived all through the winter, which Mom said was because they were in a little microclimate, protected from the cold by our house on one side catching the warmth of the sun, even in winter. How I wanted that warmth now.

While I'd been daydreaming, I'd lost the feeling in my butt. I needed to keep moving, and the only thing that made sense now was to keep going toward the moans and cries that I hoped were John-Lee.

But another fear stopped me. What if I couldn't find my way out? If I was no longer in the caves I knew, then it was quite possible, maybe even likely, that there was no exit at the end of this passage. Even if I did find John-Lee, I might only have succeeded in getting lost along with him. And if a search and rescue crew had to look for both of us, I could be the one responsible for ruining Green Mountain Academy for good.

No one would want to send their daughters to a school where a girl could sneak out in a snowstorm in the middle of the night and get trapped underground in a network of caves.

I worried that I'd done the wrong thing for the wrong reason. Heading out alone in a snowstorm had been reckless—it went against everything we'd been taught. But also, in my heart I knew that what made me take that step into the cold night was not as selfless as it seemed at first. Yes, I thought there were people who needed help. But really—if I was honest with myself—it was about making myself feel better, too. I was trying to make up for what I hadn't done to help Dad. I wanted to prove something to myself.

"Danny!" I yelled. I blew all my frustration into two piercing whistle blasts. I pushed myself onto my haunches and waited. An earthy, animal odor wafted up from beneath me. I felt a sudden need for fresh air, open space, and sun on my hair.

Music—the sound of a radio, or a phone—jingled spookily from somewhere nearby in the caves. It had not occurred to me until now that each time I blew my whistle, I was getting an answer. John-Lee was signaling me. And I was close.

I could almost recognize the song. Something Mom and Dad liked. A memory flashed into my head—a dusty road, sunshine and open windows, Mom driving, her hands pounding the steering wheel and she and Dad both singing as loud as they could. Phoebe and me in the back seat rolling our eyes and covering our ears. "Don't Stop Believin'," that was it.

With a quick inhale, I scrambled through the next opening.

The lyrics rang out clearly and I saw, at the far end of a long, narrow cave, the lit-up rectangle of a phone screen and, beside it, a huddled figure on the ground.

The beam from my headlamp landed on him and his head came up. He watched me come closer.

"John-Lee?" I called softly.

I stood in front of him, careful not to blind him with the light. He stared, not believing what he was seeing, shook his head a little, and stared some more.

"Are you John-Lee?"

"Did you fall out of a plane, too?"

"My name is Francie. I'm here to help."

"Am I dreaming?"

"No, I'm here to help you. My name is Francie." I said it again because he seemed so confused.

"But you're—Are you—? Girl, how old are you?"

"I'm thirteen."

"And I weigh a hundred and eighty pounds. How are you going to help me?"

"I haven't figured that out yet," I admitted.

He laughed a little.

"You've got to admit it's funny," he said, when I didn't laugh with him. "I fell from the sky. Miraculously, I survived that. Then I landed up in this hole, this—whatever this is, some kind of cavern? And then you materialize from the dark—a girl, and no offense, but a pretty small one at that."

I felt my temper flare. "And the award for pointing out the obvious goes to . . . ," I said, before I could stop myself.

Mom says my temper flares are a redhead thing, but I'd say this had more to do with the fact that I hadn't slept in almost twenty-four hours, I'd risked my life for this guy, I was hungry and cold, and he was insulting me.

He looked like he would laugh again, but he stopped himself. "I'm sorry."

"I'm all you have right now," I said, deliberately making my voice calmer. "I'm here and nobody else is."

"True. True," he said, and as he moved his left arm, he winced in pain. It was bent back at a weird angle and was obviously broken. "But could you tell me this one thing? Where did you come from? I have to be sure I'm not dreaming."

"You're not dreaming. I found your sister, Diamond, first."

"Diamond? Is she okay?"

"She's waiting for you in the woods. She's okay for now."

"And Rico?"

"Who's Rico?"

"Rico's the pilot."

I hesitated. "I . . . I don't know about Rico," I lied. I figured now would not be the time to tell him the bad news. "I heard about your plane disappearing. It was on the radio. I had a feeling I knew where you might be. So I came looking."

"You're some kind of clairvoyant, a psychic or something? This gets weirder and weirder. I'm dreaming, aren't I? But I can't wake up." He groaned again as he tried to shake his head.

"No, nothing like that. I live in the woods not far from here. I . . . ." There was too much to explain. And suddenly I was so tired I didn't feel like I could say another word or take another step. I threw down my backpack and sat beside him.

"Could we just focus on what to do next?" I said in a weary whisper.

"Smart. Yes. You're smart." He shifted gingerly and let out another grunt of pain he tried to cover.

"You've broken something," I said.

"My left arm, my right leg and some ribs, I think."

"Okay. I'm pretty sure I'm lost. I kept following the sounds you were making and I got turned around."

"But you're here. What did you say your name was again?"

"Francie."

"Francie, thank you for coming. I'm so glad to see you. You can't even believe how glad I am."

"But you would have been gladder if I was a one-hundred-and-eighty-pound man."

"We got off on the wrong foot. I'm not feeling quite one hundred percent. I'm not myself just now."

"Well, neither am I," I admitted.

"But you found me. You wanted to help me. That's pretty amazing."

I sniffed and didn't answer. I was trying to get my temper out of the way so I could think.

"How did *you* get here?" I said suddenly.

"I fell. Give me your light."

I handed it to him and he shone it overhead on a crack I hadn't noticed. Even with the light on it, it was hard to tell that it was an opening to the outside. The rocks were angled in such a way that they made a little slide.

"After the crash, I was crawling through the woods and the next thing I knew I woke up here. I'm not sure what I broke in the crash and what I broke falling. I guess I was unconscious for a while."

I stood up and reached for the opening. It was only about eight feet from the ground, so close, but just far enough that neither of us could reach it.

I remembered that I had water and trail mix and choco-late. I pulled them out of my backpack and handed them to John-Lee.

"I'm going to make some tea."

"What? No way. You wouldn't believe how much I've been craving a cup of hot tea."

"You need to hold your arm still. Hold it close to your body like this." I gently guided his arm.

"Uhhh!" he moaned, sounding very much like what I thought a sasquatch would sound like.

"I know it hurts." I helped him tuck it inside his jacket so it was immobilized. "Take some deep breaths."

I took out the little one-burner and set it up. The stove was smaller than a can of tuna and had legs that folded out to steady it. The fuel canister that it screwed into was about half the size of a roll of toilet paper and nearly as light.

"You know what you're doing," he said. I couldn't help but smile a little.

"You have the chocolate," he said, handing it back to me.

"No, it's for you."

"Francie, put your own mask on first."

"What does that mean?"

"It's what they say at takeoff on airplanes. If the oxygen masks drop, you're supposed to put your own on before you help someone else with theirs. It means you're my rescuer and you need to take care of yourself if you're going to help me."

"Thanks," I said, accepting the square of chocolate. He was right. Although I'd eaten the peanut butter cookie Danny had given me, I was so hungry again I was shaking. Maybe he'd noticed.

The tea water boiled almost instantly. I tossed a teabag in the little pot. I hadn't taken the time to bring sugar or milk, but anything hot would be good now.

When it was ready, I poured some into one of the plastic cups I'd brought and passed it to John-Lee. He was shaking too. I poured my own and we sat breathing in the warm steam. I thought about what we should do next.

What would Danny do after she realized she'd lost contact with me? Well, to answer that question, I just had to imagine what I'd do in her situation.

I had my answer immediately. I'd check on Diamond, then I'd hike out to meet the other girls, who by now would be on their way to find us. That's what I would do and I knew Danny would, too. She would bring them in to the crash site and to Diamond. Then they'd start looking for me and John-Lee. I had to make sure they'd find us.

CHAPTER NINETEEN

Three feet, give or take. That was all that kept me from being able to reach the rocks that would lead to the outside.

"If I could find a rock or something to boost me . . . ," I said, thinking aloud. I cast my light around the cave. Nothing looked like it would budge from the position it had probably been in for thousands of years. I tried to recall if I'd passed anything useful while crawling through the passages.

"Aren't we overlooking the obvious?" John-Lee said, swallowing the last of his tea. Even the small movement of lowering his teacup made him wince and suck in his breath.

"Which is?"

"Me. You can stand on my shoulders. Maybe that will be enough."

"What about your arm? And your leg?"

"It's not ideal, I'll grant you that. But what other choice do we have?"

I sat and stared into the darkness that was not quite total darkness; the palest blur of light filtered in through the gap above us.

"I smell something burning," John-Lee whispered.

"What?" I sniffed the air.

"It smells like . . . brain cells. I think it's coming from you." He chuckled softly. It was a good sign that he was still making jokes.

"Yeah, I'm thinking," I said. "Can you even stand up?"

"I haven't tried, to be honest. Francie?"

"Yeah?"

"Do you know what I was just thinking? I was thinking that a grown man probably wouldn't have been able to crawl through those caves like you did. He wouldn't fit."

"You're right," I said.

"So if you hadn't found me, maybe I'd never have been found. Or at least, you know, not . . . Even if we don't get out of here—"

"We're going to get out of here."

"Let's try it. It's going to hurt. But it's not going to kill me."

"Okay," I agreed.

But we didn't.

We sat there for another ten minutes or so while John-Lee shifted, trying to get in a comfortable position, and groaned softly, trying not to. He took ragged breaths. He tried to push himself up.

"You don't have to . . ." We both spoke at the same time and said the same thing.

"You go," I said.

"No, you go."

"I was just going to say you don't have to do this. I'll think of something else. I just need a minute."

"I'm not sure I can stand," he admitted. "But maybe if I kneel."

"What were you going to say?"

"Oh . . ." He sucked in his breath again and as he let it out, he cried out in pain, so sharply it made me jump.

"Try to just stay still," I said. I dug in my backpack for the blanket Danny had given me. I spread it on the damp cave floor beside John-Lee and helped him lower his body onto it. Then I pulled the remainder of the blanket up over him and tucked it around his knees.

He lay quiet for a minute, his eyes closed.

"What were you going to say?" I asked.

"Nothing."

"Nothing?"

He sighed and tensed himself against the pain. I was sure he must have broken at least one rib, maybe more.

With his eyes still closed, he said, "I was going to say you don't have to stay. But . . ."

I'd been wondering about the same thing. Was it better if I tried to find my way back through the caves to get help? Would anyone find us here, under the ground? And if they did, would it be too late?

"But . . . ?" I said.

"No," he whispered. "That's all. No 'but.'"

We sat quietly and I listened to the rasp of his breath, the howling wind and snow brushing against rock. I thought about what could happen to John-Lee if I left him.

"I'm not going anywhere," I said. "We're in this together now. I'll find a way out."

John-Lee smiled. He seemed to relax a little. Then he was asleep.

I felt suddenly alone in the echoing, shadowy cave. I was afraid I'd just made a promise I couldn't keep.

CHAPTER TWENTY

The moon's bright bright edge peeked over the mountains, then it rose quickly, spilling a silver path of light down the length of the lake. The far-shore mountains were bathed in moonglow. My canoe paddle rose, carrying a necklace of white pearls from the water. I turned to face the full moon head on, its brilliance almost blinding me.

My head fell forward and I jerked it up, then I opened my eyes.

A blinding light was shining into my eyes. But it wasn't the moon. It was a headlamp.

"Francie? Are you okay?"

The voice came to me through the fog of my dream. The light came closer and then I saw the face I would never have expected to see.

"Jasie? I thought I was in my grandma's canoe on Gem Lake." I shook my head to make sure I wasn't dreaming.

"No, it's only me," she said.

"But how did you get here? How did you find me?"

"It was Danny. She marked the spot where she last heard you. Then she came for help. We met her on the trail halfway. We were already on the way."

"Jasie, you . . ."

"And then I found an opening in the rocks under the snow, but no one could fit through it except me. Ming tied this rope to me . . ." She held it up. "I'm so glad I found you before the rope ran out or I don't know what I would have done!"

"Jasie, I can't believe it. That was so brave!"

"Who's that?" she said.

I looked over at John-Lee. He was still asleep.

"That's John-Lee. He's injured. I've been trying to figure out a way to get him out of here."

At the mention of his name, he opened his eyes. He blinked a few times. Then he said, "I was dreaming I was in a giant refrigerator. But I'd almost made it to the door. Are we getting out of here?"

"Jasie found us," I said. "We're going to help you."

He looked at both of us and closed his eyes again.

Maybe I shouldn't have taken it the way I did, but it felt like he had his doubts. Okay, I had my own doubts.

Jasie and I looked at each other. "You can't blame him," she said. "I'm not the person I'd want to see coming to my rescue either. The smallest girl in the school."

"Quit it!" I said, a flash of anger bringing heat to my face. "You said it yourself. No one else could fit through those caves. And no one else had the guts. You did it. I was running out of ideas about what to do next."

"But how will we get him out?"

"That's the problem." I showed her the gap above us. "We've got to somehow get him out that hole."

"We need help," Jasie said. "But if I crawl back out, I'm not sure I'll be able to find that hole from the outside."

"We just need to show the others where we are. I think I could hold you on my shoulders. It might be enough."

"Oh boy . . . ," Jasie said. "I don't know."

"No, I think it'll work," I said, suddenly convinced. "Here." I untied the rope from around Jasie's waist.

"If I don't start back soon, they'll try to pull on that."

"I know. Don't worry." I said it as much for myself as for her.

First, I squatted down under the hole. "They need to see your light," I said. "Climb on my shoulders." I took her hand.

"It's going to hurt you," Jasie said.

"It'll hurt. But it won't kill me." That's what John-Lee had said. If it hadn't been for his broken bones, it would have worked.

Jasie gingerly put a foot on my shoulder.

"With my boots and everything?"

"I think you need your boots. It's okay. I can take it."

I took her other hand and she hoisted herself up. She was right. It hurt. I gritted my teeth and tried to stand. As I did, I felt Jasie tilt forward a little. I tried to straighten but too late—she tumbled forward onto the ground, her headlamp rolling a few feet away.

Like a spider, she scrabbled after it, and put it back on her head.

"We almost had it!" she said excitedly. "I can't lean forward. And you have to try to stand without bending forward."

I took her hand again. She put one foot on my right shoulder. "Okay?" she said.

"Yes."

This time I made sure we both had our balance before I moved.

"Ready?"

"I'm ready."

I stood very slowly. My shoulders stung from the tread of her boots digging into my skin. But she was light and I knew I could hold her.

"Can you reach?" I asked through clenched teeth. I held onto her hands.

"I-I think so. I just—" She let go of one of my hands.

"What are you doing? Are you okay?"

I heard a clink and then, "Let me down."

We came down less carefully than we'd gone up. We landed in a tangle of arms and legs. To sit up, I had to lift Jasie's leg off my neck.

"What happened?"

"I couldn't quite reach enough to climb out."

My heart sank. I tried to hold back the disappointment I felt. I couldn't blame Jasie. If she couldn't reach, she couldn't reach.

"But," she said, scraping a chunk of mud from her thick black braid, "I turned my headlamp on flashing mode and tossed it up onto the ground outside the hole. They'll see it for sure."

"Jasie, that's brilliant!"

She shrugged and shook her head a little.

"No, really. You're smart and you're brave."

She closed her eyes, but her face in the glow of my head-lamp lit up in a smile.

CHAPTER TWENTY-ONE

Have you ever had the feeling that what's happening has already happened before? Déjà vu. The feeling swept over me as I watched the rope snake down through the crack above us and then Danny's wide-smiling face appear there.

Excited voices shouted instructions.

"Take it slow!"

"Hold on tight!"

"Check that knot!"

"You ready?"

"Everybody ready?"

Danny's face disappeared and her feet took its place. They twisted around the rope and in a few moves, she was down.

We hugged and did a little dance of joy.

"I knew you'd find me. I just didn't know if it would be—"

My voice caught. I was more tired than I'd realized.

"How is Diamond?" I asked.

"She's okay. The girls are taking care of her. You'll see. Now what are we going to do about John-Lee?"

He lay very still. Almost too still. I was worried that he'd stopped groaning. It seemed like a bad sign.

I touched my hand gently to his forehead.

"It's cool. Clammy."

"It could be shock. Or it could be just because he's lying in a cave in the middle of a snowstorm," Danny said. "Is anything broken?"

"A leg, an arm, ribs, probably."

"Whoa. We have to be careful. But we can't leave him here."

I glanced at Jasie, who had been very quiet. While I'd been watching Danny descend into the cave, Jasie had crouched on a corner of the blanket John-Lee lay on. Her arms wrapped around her knees, but that didn't stop her whole body from quaking with shivering.

"Jasie, are you okay?"

She went to speak, but dropped her chin to her knees to try to steady her chattering teeth. Her lips were purplish. She didn't answer.

Danny immediately stripped off her parka and wrapped it around Jasie tenderly. Like a dreamer wakened from sleep, Jasie tried to fight her off, mumbling incoherently.

"Ming!" I called up through the gap. "We need to get Jasie out. And we need a parka for Danny."

In the light I saw Ming fighting with something bulky. Then her own parka dropped through the hole.

Tears choked my throat. A warm glow of pride swelled in my chest; these brave girls were my friends, almost my family. I couldn't speak, but I helped Danny into the parka. She accepted it without question. The girls would work it out and find another for Ming, but Danny and I both knew that to help Jasie and John-Lee, we needed to look after ourselves, too.

The rope disappeared up through the hole and Grace's voice came to us.

"Can she stand up by herself?"

"Can you stand?" I asked Jasie.

Her soft brown eyes met mine. But she didn't need to say anything for me to have my answer.

"No!" I called back.

"Okay, hang on."

Danny and I helped Jasie to a spot just below the hole.

"I'll get you to tie a bowline around Jasie."

Grace lowered the rope. "Ming will walk you through it just to be sure."

Now Ming's face appeared again. She was wearing someone else's parka.

"Loop it under her armpits. Now make your loop."

Danny took off her gloves and flipped the rope in a loop over itself.

"Good. Leave enough of a tail."

I watched Danny's hands, trembling slightly, as they followed Ming's instructions. Snow continued to sprinkle down through the hole, coating all three of us in a crust of ice crystals.

"That's right," she encouraged Danny. "Now finish it off with a double overhand."

My own teeth had begun to chatter noisily. None of us could stay down in this cave much longer.

When the rope was secure around Jasie's armpits, they began to pull her up. Danny and I guided her body, hanging onto her feet until she was out of reach.

She was in other hands now and I knew the girls would take good care of her.

"Jumping jacks," Danny said.

"What?"

"Come on. Do some with me. You're shivering like a chipmunk."

As tired as I was, as much as I wanted to curl into a ball under a blanket, I knew Danny was right. The worst thing we could do right now would be to stop moving.

"How are you two?" Grace called down as we flung our arms out and back, out and back. "We've got tea, cookies, sandwiches . . . What do you need?"

"Let's just get this done," I said.

"Fine. But if I see any sign you're getting hypothermic, I'm coming down there."

John-Lee was not an eighty-pound girl. Getting him out would not be so simple.

In a couple of minutes, Ming was back. She lowered herself down the hole. Grace dropped two long, straight pine branches they'd found in the woods down after her, followed by a plastic tarp.

Ming and Danny spread out the tarp.

"We need to gently roll him onto the tarp," Ming said, moving quickly.

As we did, he opened his eyes and looked at me.

"We're getting you out," I said through my chattering teeth.

Ming and Danny laid a pole on each side of the tarp. Not glancing up from her task, Ming said, "You need to get warm, too, Francie."

"I told John-Lee I'd stay with him."

They rolled the tarp around the pine poles toward each other and stopped at John-Lee's sides.

When that was done, John-Lee was in a makeshift stretcher. Danny and I got on the heavy end with his head and shoulders, Ming on the foot end, and we carried him over to the hole.

Working expertly, Ming looped the rope over John-Lee and the stretcher in two places and secured it tightly.

"Ready!" she called up to Grace.

"Ready!" Grace called back, and John-Lee, safe in his stretcher, began to rise up toward the gap.

CHAPTER TWENTY-TWO

Muffled voices, like a brook burbling softly over stones. A warm cocoon wrapped tightly around me. Arms lifting me. The weightless feeling of being carried through the dark.

Time confused—how old was I? Mom carrying me from the car, my sleepy head rolling on her shoulder, the car door clicks closed behind her, a rectangle of light at the top of the steps and Dad's silhouette standing there, his arms out.

Next time I opened my eyes, a warm orange glow danced on a tarp overhead. A large fire snapped and spit not far from my feet. Its warmth radiated through my body, warming my feet, my fingers. The girls' voices murmured softly. I felt so safe and comfortable. I didn't ever want to move from this soft warm nest—where? In among the fragrant pines. When I shifted, a smell like Christmas wafted up.

Beyond the fire and the silhouettes of the girls sitting around it, a bright moon hung in the sky. There was no wind, I realized. The storm had passed finally. I propped myself up on my elbow. Beside me lay another sleeping bag cocoon—John-Lee, I saw.

"Where's Diamond?" I said.

"You're awake," said Danny.

"I'm right here, Franny," Diamond said, and I saw her then. A blanket was wrapped around her shoulders as she sat by the fire. "Your friends have fixed me up." She showed me her leg secured in a brace made of branches and tied with scarves.

"Where's Jasie?"

"Ming and Grace took her back on a stretcher," said Danny. "They tried to warm her up, but they felt like it would be better to get her to the school as soon as possible."

"Is she—?"

"We don't know," said Carmen.

I didn't know what to say. It couldn't happen. It couldn't happen that Jasie would be in danger because she had saved me.

"And John-Lee?" I looked over at him.

"We have to get him out, too. But we'll wait for Ming and Grace."

"You just need to stay warm. That's your job now," Carmen said. She got up from the fire and handed me a cup of steaming hot chocolate. "Drink this. We're looking after things."

She explained the plan to me.

While the rescue was going on, Carmen and Lindsay had put together this camp in a clearing close to the cave. They'd built a quick lean-to with a large tarp and some strong rope and covered the floor of it with spruce and fir boughs. Another tarp was laid on top of that and they made our beds on it. Then they'd built up a good fire in front of the lean-to entrance so it radiated heat into it. More spruce and fir boughs lay around the fire for seats. They'd helped Diamond to sit beside it and made a brace for her leg.

Meredith had stayed back at the school with Ms. B to prepare food for when we returned and to try and make contact with someone if the power came back on.

The idea was to take back the injured first, on a sled that Grace and Ming would bring with them when they came.

Just then Lindsay came tromping into the circle of light from the fire, dragging some long branches for fuel.

"Francie! You're awake," she called. "No sign of Grace and Ming?"

"Not yet," said Carmen.

In the soft roar of the fire, we were all silent, each lost in her own worries. Jasie was the biggest worry. The smallest girl in the school and she had stepped out onto the thin limb of her own fears, not once, but twice. She'd been alone in the fire tower as the storm raged and probably shuddered the timbers of the tower and she had kept a vigil for me and for Danny. I could picture her squinting against the flying snow, sending the beam of her flashlight up into the dizzying whirl of white.

As if reading my mind, Danny spoke from the edge of the fire.

"You should have seen Jasie. She noticed a little dip in the snow, like a funnel. It was a tiny crack that only she could have fit down. We didn't even know for sure where it would lead. She said, 'I bet this is part of the cave system she's in.' Meaning you, Francie. She said, 'I can go down there.'

"Grace, you know Grace, she said, 'That's a stupid idea. Like we're going to send you down there alone.' And then Ming said, 'Wait. Maybe there's a way.' We had no other ideas. So Ming tied the rope around her and she just did it. I was so impressed."

"Little Jasie," Lindsay said, her voice holding a touch of awe. "She was amazing."

We fell silent again. I sipped my hot chocolate, the mug warm in my hands.

Jasie's parents were far away, in Burkina Faso. Would they need to come home if——? I could hardly let my mind think it. Even if she recovered, would they pull her out of the school when they heard what happened? This could be the reason the school closed down for good.

What about the rest of us? Danny's mom, as chief financial officer of their First Nation, traveled often. At those times, Danny either had to stay home alone or stay with cousins. But also, she said that if she wasn't at Green Mountain Academy, she'd have to go to school in town. And it was a forty-five-minute bus ride each way.

As for me, there were two choices, both of them bad: live with Grandpa and his moods or move to the city with Aunt Sissy and live in an apartment on the tenth floor, where when you looked out the window, all you saw was other apartments. In fact, you didn't even need to look out——the windows of the other buildings looked in on you: people in their kitchens making dinner, TVs on, or lit but empty rooms that felt like unblinking eyes, waiting for something. Aunt Sissy said it didn't bother her. She was used to it.

Last time I visited her, a weekend was enough for me. The view *was* beautiful. At night I could see the lights on Grouse Mountain across the city and the lit-up dome of Science World; in the daytime, boats and water taxis crossed False Creek like toys. But I couldn't wait until breakfast was over and we could *get out*. After coming down the elevator and crossing the mirrored lobby, we stepped out into the street and I took in a huge gulp of fresh air like I'd been holding my breath.

Aunt Sissy laughed. "Feeling a bit claustrophobic?" she said.

"I guess," I said, not wanting to tell her the truth. I felt suffocated. I wanted to run, climb a tree, listen to the silence.

"You can do all that in Vancouver," she told me another day, when we were discussing what she called "my options." "Vancouver is an outdoorsy city. Two minutes from here and you're on the ocean in your kayak."

"I guess," I said. Maybe it was all in my head. But the problem for me was not being able to just step out the door and be gone into the woods.

Breathing in the cold, piney air around me now, I couldn't believe how quickly my mind had gone from worrying about Jasie to worrying about myself. I felt ashamed.

At that moment, John-Lee groaned. Diamond tried to get up, awkward in her leg brace, but Carmen stopped her. "I'll go," she said. She jumped up and came over to him in the lean-to.

"Try not to move," she told him. "You're safe. You'll be out of here soon."

"What's taking them so long?" Lindsay said softly to Danny.

Diamond's anxious eyes met mine.

"Let's sing something for John-Lee," she said.

"'Catch Me'!" said Lindsay. "We know all the words."

So as the moon sank behind the trees and the fire shape-shifted, rising, twisting, turning, Diamond sang and our voices joined hers, sending a message ringing through the forest—we are still here.

CHAPTER TWENTY-THREE

We heard them first—the distinct crunch of boots in the snow. Then their light bobbed through the trees and we all let out shouts of relief.

"They're back!"

"Finally!"

"We're getting out of here."

"How's Jasie?" Carmen called as Ming and Grace stepped into the firelight.

They stole a quick look at each other before Grace answered. "She's not good."

"The power's not back on yet and it'll probably be a few hours before it is," Ming added. "The driveway is completely plugged with a giant snowdrift, so there's no driving out or in until we get a tractor in to clear it. We can't contact anyone."

"What are we going to do?" Lindsay asked.

"I. Don't. Know," Grace said, her voice hard. "Do any of you have any good ideas? We're miles from anything—we're in the wilderness, in case you hadn't noticed."

"Grace," said Ming softly.

"Everybody knew what they were signing up for when they came to this school. It's a *wilderness* school; that's the idea. And now you're all chickening out?"

"Nobody's chickening out," Lindsay said. "I just asked what we were going to do."

"Well how should I know? Since when am I in charge?"

"Nobody said you were."

"It's starting to feel that way."

"Listen, girls," Diamond began.

But Grace's anger marched right over her voice. "This school has been everything to me. It's the only family I've got. It's my home. And now I'm going to lose it all."

There was silence, but the air rang with her words and seemed to echo from the trees and rocks like a chorus.

"I don't know what you mean by that," Lindsay said quietly. "I don't know what you're losing. I mean, what? The school? Nobody's going anywhere. We're still here."

Grace shook her head angrily. In the firelight, her face looked twisted, like she might cry. I had never seen Grace cry.

"You really don't get it? The school was on the brink of closing already. There's not enough students. Nine girls."

"Eight," Lindsay said.

"Eight. Okay, if you must remind me, Lindsay. Eight girls. I mean, where do you think the money's coming from to keep the lights on and feed us every day? You, Carmen, Ming. You have no idea what it's like to have nowhere else to go." She looked over at me and Danny, but didn't include us.

"Well, wait a minute," Carmen said. "What are we even talking about now?"

"You all know the school's broke!" Grace shouted. She sat down heavily beside the fire. "Now this. This'll be all over the news. The school is finished. You might as well start packing your bags."

A giant ember popped from the fire and landed in the snow at Grace's feet. She stomped on it.

"You know," Diamond said. "You girls must be exhausted. You've been up all night. Things can look impossible at night. 'Weeping may tarry for the night, but joy comes with the morning.'"

"*The Jungle Book*," said Lindsay.

Everyone turned to look at her. "Things will look better in the morning. That's what Bagheera says to Mowgli."

"There you go," said Diamond. "Wisdom for the ages."

"Anyway," said Ming. "It's not helping anything to worry about things that haven't even happened yet."

"Don't borrow trouble," Danny said. "My grandma."

Diamond's musical laugh broke out and echoed in the dark. "Wise words!" she said.

But even her bright laughter couldn't erase the gloom of Grace's words. I didn't think the others knew what Danny and I knew from Lucy's email. Unless a miracle happened and Lucy and Lill found a way to bring in more students—and I had no idea how that was supposed to happen—the school was going to shut down. Their brother Larry had said so. Before Christmas, he'd said. We'd be home before Christmas.

I know Christmas is supposed to be the greatest thing—even for people who aren't religious, as our family wasn't, and even for some people who have other traditions and celebrate it just as a fun holiday. But Christmas had stopped being fun for me a long time ago.

Once, it was magical. I think of it as always Christmas Eve, Phoebe and me in our new flannel pajamas that we were always allowed to open that night. They had a fresh smell like candy canes. Hoping to catch a glimpse of Santa's sleigh, we hung over the back of the couch and looked out the picture window at moonlight sparkling on snow. Christmas-tree smell filled our small house, Mom in the cramped den with the door closed, the sound of crinkling wrapping paper and scissors slicing through paper, and occasionally a swear word.

She wasn't good at wrapping. It was a family joke. Dad's wrapping was neat and precise with crisp, tucked edges and Santa faces or kittens lined up so they appeared whole. Mom's wrapping was a bumpy, bunched-up bulge, sometimes twisted like a firecracker on two ends, way too much tape and often patched together with two kinds of paper.

Dad teased her gently. "Oh, look at that! One of the reindeers must have wrapped this one!"

Phoebe and I had snickered. Even at five years old, we only half-believed in all of that. But we wanted to believe. And late at night, too excited to sleep, we lay awake and whispered to each other and then we heard tapping on the roof. Our bedroom door creaked open and Dad's head appeared in the crack of light.

"Did you hear that?"

"Yes!" we both said in one excited breath.

"Better get to sleep quick then," he said.

After Phoebe died, all the magic was gone out of Christmas, not just for me but for Mom and Dad too. The sounds then from the den were not swear words, but Mom's stifled sobs as Dad and I sat at the round dining room table picking at store-bought cookies and trying not to look at each other. The lump in my throat, the knot cinched around my heart has never totally gone away.

CHAPTER TWENTY-FOUR

While I'd been daydreaming, Grace had moved away from the fire and was working on fitting the sled to carry the injured back to the school. The cordless drill bore into the quiet of the forest. Danny and Ming jumped up to help her and the rest of us sat and waited. Diamond began to sing again, more quietly, almost to herself, a haunting song I didn't know.

I felt the cold more now. John-Lee cried out softly and shifted in his sleeping bag.

"Francie?" he whispered.

"I'm right here."

"This is my fault."

"What do you mean? Nothing's your fault."

"Yes, yes, listen." The sleeping bag rustled with his movement and he tried to muffle his ragged groans.

"Stay still!" I whispered back. "You'll be out of here soon. A few more minutes."

"No, listen. Where is Rico? I was the one who wanted to fly tonight. Diamond wanted to wait. Rico said he'd do what we wanted. I was the one who pushed it. It's my fault. Where is he? I know why you're not—"

His voice caught as he stifled another gasp of pain.

What should I tell him? Was it right to keep lying to him about the pilot?

"Our concert in Seattle. That's all I cared about," he said. "And now Rico—"

I didn't know what to say. I knew what it felt like to blame yourself. Would Phoebe have died if I had acted differently? That day in the woods beside Gem Lake. We'd been playing hide-and-seek. Phoebe wasn't allowed to run because Mom was worried about her heart condition. But I'd already lost twice and so I'd cheated, weaving at full speed through the trees when she wasn't looking. She caught me and dug deep, the way she sometimes did, to find something to say that would hurt me. She knew just where to look.

"You've got skinny legs," she said.

"I do not."

It was something the bigger boys at school teased me about and she knew it.

"Yes you do. I don't know how you can even walk, let alone run."

I took the bait. That's what Mom would say.

"You can't run at all," I shot back.

That had been enough to spur Phoebe on, and she *had* run, she'd run like the wind, like a deer bounding over deadfall and rocks. She was like lightning. I wish I could have told her so. But I never did.

Things happened one after another, tumbling along like duck feathers in the wind, rolling across the surface of the lake. Phoebe went into the hospital and she never came out. It was not my fault. It was not because she'd been running. Everyone told me that. I wished I could believe it.

Give up all hope of a better past, Grandma used to say. In my better past, I would not have taken the bait. I would have understood how hard it was for Phoebe to be constantly watched by Mom, when even the doctor was not so cautious, how it felt to always be left out of things, to be asked how she was feeling. In my better past, I wouldn't have cheated. I would have said, "I like my skinny legs just fine," and then Phoebe would have laughed and we would have crawled into the fort we made and checked to see how many pine cones we had saved in our pine cone stash.

And then there was Dad's hat by the creek in the Oregon woods. If I had crossed the creek that night. If I had kept looking for him. There was a chance I could have found him.

I tried to think of some wise words to say to John-Lee. "It's not your fault," was all I said, echoing what had been said to me back then. But I knew from his silence that the words meant no more to him than they did to me.

"We're ready for you," Grace said, her dark shape silhouetted against the orange light of the fire. She pulled the sled in close. She'd added boards to it to make it longer and sides so that they could immobilize John-Lee. She, Ming and Danny bent to John-Lee where he lay on the tree boughs.

"All hands on deck," Grace said. "Everyone who can walk. Not you, Francie."

"Take Diamond first," John-Lee whispered.

"You don't get a say," Grace said. "We're taking people in the order of most injured first. It's only logical."

"I weigh a hundred and eighty pounds. How are you girls going to get me over all those rocks?"

"We've had practice," Ming said. "We've portaged a few canoes over worse terrain."

"Do you want to stay with Francie and Diamond?" Carmen asked Danny.

I saw her hesitate. She wanted to help with the rescue.

"I'm okay," I said. "We'll be fine. You go ahead."

"You're sure?" Danny said. "I can stay."

"I'm sure."

"You're shivering," said Carmen. "Come on. Move around a bit. Then sit by the fire with Diamond."

I wriggled out of my sleeping bag cocoon and I did as she said, windmilling my arms and shaking out each leg as the girls carefully lifted John-Lee into the sled. They packed the sleeping bag around him and Ming tied him in snugly.

"Francie!" John-Lee spoke.

I moved closer.

"Thank you," he said.

CHAPTER TWENTY-FIVE

I opened one eye and saw the cozy fire crackling in the fire-place. Sleeping bags bulky with sleeping girls lay in front of it. But daylight had lightened the room.

We had made it through the night. Cobwebs of wind-whipped snow piled in the corners of the windowpanes. The smell of coffee and cinnamon filled the air.

Sitting up, I turned to see Ms. B tending the coffee percola-tor on the great room woodstove. When she saw me, she smiled, but it was a sad smile. Then she put her finger to her lips.

The couches had been pushed aside and three cots had been set up in a row behind the sleeping bags. They held Jasie, John-Lee and Diamond. In a chair beside Jasie's cot, Meredith sat, looking nearly asleep, her chin resting on her chest. On one of the coffee tables pulled up next to her was a mug, a thermom-eter and the first aid book. The mug gave me hope. If Jasie was able to drink liquids for herself, that would be a good sign.

Then I noticed Lilac. Curled in a circle, she had nestled into the blankets close to Jasie's body.

Ms. B came over with two hot water bottles.

"Meredith," she whispered, bending to her ear.

"Oh, what time is it?" Meredith said, rousing herself with a start. She pushed herself up and leaned over to Jasie, putting her hand in front of Jasie's mouth. I knew what she was doing. She was trying to see if she was still breathing.

Tears burbled in my throat as I tried to breathe myself. I slipped out of my sleeping bag and went over to them.

"How is she?" I asked.

"I'm just changing these hot water bottles. Lilac, out of the way." Meredith nudged the cat gently. Lilac reluctantly got up, moving just down the blankets to sit and watch. It was as if she knew something was wrong.

Meredith drew back the heavy wool blankets and pulled out the two hot water bottles and handed them to Ms. B. Then she tucked the fresh warm ones close in to Jasie's tiny body. She looked so frail suddenly. It seemed impossible that such a small girl had done this brave thing on such a cold and stormy night.

When she'd retucked the blankets snugly and Lilac's soft white and orange body had settled back down close to Jasie, Meredith met my eyes.

"She hasn't woken up. That's the worry. Her temperature is slowly getting better, but she seems to be unconscious. There's nothing more we can do for her. She needs to get to a hospital."

"We have to go for help," I said.

Ms. B shook her head. "I can't let anyone else put themselves at risk. I'd go myself if I thought I had any chance of making it."

Everyone knew that wasn't an option. I'd never learned what was wrong with Ms. B, but I'd heard the sisters discussing her "mobility issues," as they called them. Basically, Ms. B couldn't walk very far or even be on her feet for too long before she needed to sit down and rest.

"I can go," I said, a bit louder than I meant to. "I've rested more than the others. It should be me."

"Forget it!" Grace's voice came from behind me. "You've done enough damage. No one's going anywhere."

"What are you talking about?" Carmen said, also sitting up. "How can you say that?"

"That's unfair," Ming added, her voice calm but firm.

All the girls were suddenly awake and sitting up in a confusion of rustling sleeping bags and voices.

Danny spoke. "Francie's right. Someone has to go. It could be hours before the power comes back on. Even days. Jasie can't wait that long and neither can John-Lee and Diamond."

"I'm okay," John-Lee said. His deep voice sounded strange in a house used to girls' voices.

"You're not okay," Diamond said. "But I am. I can hold out and wait. I'm not sure I get a vote, but from what I've seen, these girls are more than capable. If they think they should go for help, well, I for one am not going to argue with them."

At that, Ms. B seemed thoughtful, like she might agree. She and Meredith looked at each other as if considering.

Grace said, "It's not about being capable or not. This school is in deep trouble. You all seem to think what Francie and Danny and Jasie did was some great heroic move. Well, it wasn't! It was stupid and risky. It's amazing no one got killed." She glanced over at Jasie and added, "Yet."

"It put everybody in danger," she went on. "And trying to fix it now by sending someone else out into danger is just going to make it worse."

Everyone was quiet. I could almost see the wheels turning in Ms. B's head, and in Meredith's. Jasie lay as still as death. We could hear Lilac's loud purr as she lay beside her.

"There's something to what Grace says," Lindsay said, breaking the silence. "The snow out there is very deep. If someone goes, they'll have to walk at least twenty kilometers. Once they get out there, there'll be no turning back. It *is* dangerous. Lucy and Lill will be trying to do everything they can to get back. Maybe it's best to just wait for them."

"Well, I don't know," said Carmen. "I can see both sides. Let's vote on it."

John-Lee cleared his throat. "Wait. Can I say something? Like Diamond said, I don't have a right to vote on this. But what you girls did, yeah, it was risky—no doubt about it. Brave? Are you kidding me? I've never seen braver. And *it saved my life*. Mine and probably Diamond's too. If it wasn't for you girls—"

He choked up, caught his breath, then continued. "And I could be wrong, but from what I gather, this school, what you're all doing here, well, isn't it about survival? Didn't you all just do what you've been training to do? You don't learn survival skills to stay in the house. Am I right? As for me, if you vote, I'm going to abstain. I don't get a say in this."

"Me too," said Diamond. "This is for you girls to decide."

"Who said we're voting?" said Grace. "I'm the oldest. I've been here the longest. I've got the most experience and I say we stay put."

"I think we should vote," said Ming. "This is too big a decision for one person."

"My aunts run this school!" Grace said. She was on her feet now, her short blonde hair a wild mess, half sticking to her cheek, half sticking out porcupine-quill straight.

"Who wants to vote?" said Carmen.

Everyone but Grace, John-Lee, Diamond and Ms. B put up their hands.

"You're voting on voting? Idiotic," said Grace.

"Well, you can—what was that word John-Lee said?" Carmen asked.

"Abstain," said Ming.

"You can abstain if you want."

Grace made a noise of disgust. I felt bad for her. She was used to Lindsay and Carmen being on her side as the oldest girls. She was used to her word being the final word.

"Who votes to stay here and wait?" asked Carmen. She looked sideways at Grace and seemed uncertain.

Only Grace and Lindsay put up their hands.

"And who votes we walk out?"

Carmen slowly put up her hand. So did I, Danny, Ming and Meredith.

"So it's decided," Ming said. "We walk out."

"Girls," Ms. B spoke up. "I respect your vote. Grace, you're right, you're the oldest. I respect that, too. You have the most experience. But I'm the one in charge. Vote or not, what I say goes."

Everyone held their breath, watching as her worried face pondered the decision. She turned away and picked up the coffee pot, poured a stream of steaming coffee into a mug. She stood for a moment with her back to us, her head bent over the coffee cup. Then she turned to all of us.

"Yes, it's dangerous. But so is doing nothing. Jasie's life is in danger. I agree with the vote."

"You've all just put the nail in the coffin of this school," Grace said, throwing a log on the fire with too much force. "I hope you're happy."

CHAPTER TWENTY-SIX

Snowflakes floated down softly in the morning air as Danny, Ming and I strapped on our snowshoes. Lindsay had made a path to the shed and dug out the snow shovel and was now clearing the porch of what looked like about a foot and a half of snow.

Each of us wore a daypack with the lunches that Ms. B had made—peanut butter and banana sandwiches, oatmeal cookies, oranges and hot tea in thermoses. Ming had Ms. B's cell phone in case we got lucky and picked up a signal partway down the hill.

We would be walking downhill, toward the farmhouse that was about twenty kilometers away. Uphill, there was nothing, just a logging road that went deep into thick bush. Downhill, if no one was home at the first house, we'd have another couple kilometers to the next place. If we walked long enough, we'd get to town. But we hoped it wouldn't come to that.

Our snowshoes sank into the soft snow, but it was better than walking in only boots, which would have been much slower. We trudged along in silence, listening to birds twittering happily in the trees, the crunch of our footsteps in the snow and the squeak of Ming's snowshoe bindings.

She stopped to adjust the straps and Danny and I breathed in the clean, fresh air. We could almost imagine it was a normal day.

When we started to walk again, Danny said, to no one in particular, "Do you think Grace is right? Is the school going to close?"

We walked a few minutes more before Ming said, "Whether she's right or not, that can't be the reason we don't go for help. It's the right thing to do."

"I know," said Danny.

A set of animal tracks dotted the snow across our path and disappeared into the woods.

"Rabbit?" said Danny.

"I think so," said Ming.

We walked for a few more minutes and came to the fallen pine tree, covered in snow now, which had taken the power line down. The other toppled trees had created a little snowy valley. We straddled the downed tree and kept walking.

Then Danny's left foot sank in deeper than her right and she fell on her knees into the deep snow. I caught her arm and helped her up.

"Brush the snow off," said Ming. "It's warming up. We don't want our clothes wet if we can help it."

Her snowshoe came up carrying a load of snow on the tip and she kicked it off.

"We have to find a way to keep the school open," Danny said firmly. "Our school. It's Lill's and Lucy's, they started it, but it's ours now too. Other than home, it's the only place I feel like I can be myself. We should be able to do something."

I could tell Ming wanted to say something, but she kept quiet. The snow was getting heavier. When we lifted our feet, clumps of snow stuck to the snowshoes. We broke branches off a dead tree and used them to try to clear the sticky snow from the shoes.

"I feel the same as you, Danny," Ming said after a few minutes. "I can be myself out here, and at this school. But the school's had problems for a while. Grace, Carmen, Lindsay, we all know about it. They need more students—it's that simple."

She knocked a chunk of snow off her shoe. "Anyway, that's why Grace is so upset. She thinks this is the last straw."

"The nail in the coffin," said Danny.

"I'll be honest," Ming said. "I think it was already too late to save the school. And believe me, the last thing I want is to go back to Vancouver. I'll have to go to the private school that my dad wanted me to go to in the first place. I'll have to wear a stupid uniform. And I'll have to save my fingers for piano, not rock climbing. It was only because of my mom that I got to come here. If I go back to Vancouver, I can forget about becoming a pro climber."

"Wait," said Danny. "Wait. What is that? Do you hear that?"

We stood in the road and listened. The snow curled down lazily. From somewhere down the road, a raven cawed.

"That?" said Ming.

"No."

A few more ravens joined in a sudden ruckus and then I did hear it—a high bellow like some kind of charging moose or elephant.

"Snowmobiles!" said Danny.

"Snowmobiles!" Ming and I shouted.

"Let's hurry."

We plunged forward, lifting our heavy feet, legs straining. Danny took the lead and Ming and I followed, literally in her footsteps, which made our progress a bit easier.

Ahead, we saw another big tree that had come down in the storm, this one caught up in the power line like an arrow resting on a bow. Two snowmobiles roared up to it and stopped. The riders shut off their engines and climbed off the machines.

"Hello!" Danny yelled.

Their heads came up in surprise. The three of us jog-shuffled the rest of the way down to them.

"Where are you coming from?" one of them asked. She was dressed in an orange and black BC Hydro parka with the fur-trimmed hood cinched close around her helmet. She loosened the hood and pulled off her helmet. "Warming up," she said.

"Last thing I expected to come across out here," the man said.

"We're from the school up the hill. Green Mountain Academy," said Ming. "We need help. We've got three injured people."

"We've got a radio," said the woman, reaching for the mic clipped to her parka. "Injured how?"

"You heard about the missing airplane?" I asked.

They just stared at us, not understanding.

"We found the plane," I said.

CHAPTER TWENTY-SEVEN

A giant dragonfly with a delicate body kicked up a mist of snow then touched down in the open area in front of Green Mountain Academy.

All of us watched from the porch as two paramedics jumped from the helicopter. They hauled out a stretcher and gear and moved smoothly through the door to where Ms. B directed them, to Jasie.

They were kind, but efficient, checking her heart, her eyes. Then they packed her warmly and securely and carried her out. John-Lee was next, squeezing my hand as they loaded him onto the stretcher. Diamond stopped to kiss Danny and me, then she limped out herself, wrapped in the gray flannel blanket they'd given her, with her hand on the paramedic's arm for support.

The rotors of the helicopter *chop-chopped* back to life and then the dragonfly lifted and rose, tipping forward slightly then ascending into the sky, the noise fading as it gained altitude. It glided over the trees and disappeared.

Relief mixed with a sick feeling. The scene rippled before my eyes like something underwater.

"Are you okay?" Danny whispered, grabbing my hand.

"I'm-I'm just—"

"You're pale. Come and sit down." She guided me to the couch in front of the fire. "They're taking care of everything now. Everything's going to be okay."

She tucked the wool couch throw around our legs. Lilac left her place on Jasie's cot and jumped up to join us. Grace carried in an armload of wood and the sound it made as it landed in the almost empty wood box was comforting. It was the same sound we heard on Saturday nights when we played cards around the table, glasses of lemonade and bowls of chips and pretzels beside us, a cool gust of air wafting in the door as someone brought in wood to last the night; the same sound we heard when we stomped off our boots on the mat, our cheeks warm after a good long hike. It was the sound of safety.

Grace added a log to the fire and stirred it with the poker, bringing the dancing flames back to life. She had been quiet since the rescue, not willing to admit that maybe she'd been wrong, that maybe hiking out had been the right idea after all. But since we were all waiting to find out about Jasie, no one was celebrating yet.

"I'm making chicken stew," called Ms. B as she headed to the kitchen. "I expect Lill and Lucy will be home tomorrow."

Next to Ms. B's spaghetti, Ms. B's chicken stew was our favorite.

"I'll make biscuits," said Meredith. "I'm getting pretty good at using this woodstove." Ms. B's chicken stew with Meredith's biscuits was even better.

Lindsay and Carmen stripped the bedding from John-Lee's and Diamond's cots and folded it up. The busy sounds closed over the emptiness of the helicopter leaving, the emptiness of Jasie's cot, with its thick layers of blankets turned back like pages in a half-read book.

"You okay?" said Danny again.

I nodded. But I wasn't so sure I was. Everything seemed to be going back to normal. Except it wasn't. I wondered if there was such a thing as normal. Maybe my problem was trying to pretend there was.

❖

About halfway through dinner, the lights came back on.

"Hey!" everyone cried at once.

"I'm sort of sorry," said Meredith. "I was starting to like living by candlelight."

"Well, it means we can get a message to the sisters," said Lindsay.

"Oh, yeah. Let's see if we can get them on an internet call," Carmen said, jumping up. "I'll reset the modem."

"Carmen, finish your stew," Ms. B said calmly. "They're probably on their way right now."

Later, as we cleaned up the dishes, Carmen and Grace tried to get the internet back online. But they weren't getting a signal.

"We'll have to climb up and check the satellite dish," said Grace. "It probably got knocked off-kilter in the storm."

"It's dark," said Ms. B. "I think this should wait till morning."

"It should," said Carmen, playfully throwing an arm around Ms. B's shoulders. "But you know us girls. We don't always follow the 'shoulds.'"

Ms. B laughed; like the rest of us, she was eager to get a message to the sisters. "Well for heaven's sake, be careful," she said.

"Where's the ladder?" Carmen said.

"It's in the shed," said Lindsay. "I saw it in there when I was getting the shovel."

After dishes were done, we sat on the floor in front of the fire eating oranges and sipping mint tea. Meredith and Ming played cribbage, but Danny and I were both too tired to do much of anything.

Grace, Carmen and Lindsay had just come back in laughing and trying to hide the snowballs they carried. The happy, open look on Grace's face reminded me of what she'd said. This was her only family. Carmen pitched a snowball into the nest of blankets. Then the lights went out again.

"Hey!"

"What the heck?"

"Oh brother, not again."

"That's it for me. I'm going to bed," Ms. B said.

Danny and I decided it was warm enough to sleep in our room. My body ached from being cold and sleeping on the ground. I wanted my bed. We carried our sleeping bags, still toasty from being near the fire, and piled them on our beds.

It was good to be safe and warm again. It was good to have everything in its proper place. Almost everything.

Lilac had followed us into our room and now she jumped onto the end of my bed and kneaded her paws against my blankets. I couldn't bear to think of Jasie waking up alone in the hospital, that she might cry for Lilac. But it was even worse to think she might not wake up at all.

In the middle of the night, I opened my eyes suddenly to find our alarm clock had come back on and was blinking a beam of red light into the darkness. The power was back.

"You awake?" Danny's voice came from her bed.

"Yeah."

"I can't stop thinking about the pilot. Maybe if I hadn't tried to stop you from going, if we had got there sooner—I was just being selfish. I could hear my uncle scolding me. I was just afraid."

I reached over and punched the button to stop the time from blinking.

"There's no way the pilot could have survived," I said. "We wouldn't have saved him."

"Do you think so?"

"I'm sure of it. It's not your fault," I said.

It was the same thing I'd said to John-Lee, and it was true. But somehow we all had a way of telling ourselves stories that could bloom like flowers or spread like weeds. And once those stories started to grow, it was hard to stop them.

CHAPTER TWENTY-EIGHT

Worry was written on Lucy's and Lill's faces like the long blue shadows of the aspens falling on fresh snow in the yard the afternoon they finally arrived home. Flights had been delayed in the clean-up after the storm. We were so happy to see them drive up, we all spilled into the yard, kicking up snow in arcs that showered down, sparkling in the sunlight. They handed off their bags to Grace and Lindsay, hugged Ms. B, and laughed with us.

"It's good to be home," Lucy said, smiling.

"It sure is," said Lill.

"I saved you chicken stew," Ms. B said, leading the way to the porch.

We would have dinner together around the big table and hear their stories and tell them ours. But the dark shadows in their faces were impossible to ignore. A cloud had descended on Green Mountain Academy and all our usual activities felt heavier, like we were moving through an invisible gray fog, just waiting for the raincloud to burst open.

Then their brother Larry arrived.

"You came all the way from Toronto. We're not going to spend your whole visit inside behind closed doors having gloomy discussions." I heard Lill talking to him as I came into the kitchen the morning after his arrival.

Lill poured coffee into two mugs while Larry buttered toast.

"Well, it's not exactly party time around here," he said.

"You know what I mean. Your last visit was so short. When's the last time you were out in the woods?"

"It's been a while," he admitted. "It's such a hassle to get out of the city. And I work pretty much twelve hours a day, sometimes more. When I get a moment to myself, I'm too tired to go anywhere. I just sit on the couch and watch football or basketball, or whatever is on."

"You used to love the woods."

"I know. I still do, I guess. It feels good to be out here again."

I reached around him to get the cereal bowls down.

"You're the girl who found the plane, aren't you?" he said.

I didn't answer.

"I heard you knew where to look. You went out there all by yourself."

"This is Francie Fox," said Lill.

"I heard it was out in the Giant's Lair," he said. "How did you know it would be there?"

"The Giant's Lair?" said Lill.

"That's what we used to call those caves."

"I'd forgotten about that."

I stood there holding the cereal bowls as Larry waited for me to say something.

"I . . . ," I began. There was too much to explain. It hadn't been like that. I'd gone blindly, stupidly. The plane had led me to it, not the other way around. I'd put everybody in danger. Like Grace said, we'd been lucky; I'd been lucky. But somehow it had turned into this story where I actually knew what I was doing.

There was an awkward silence as I struggled to find the words.

"Well," Larry said, breaking it. "It must have been scary. I'm impressed."

He stuck out his hand to shake mine, and there was another awkward moment as I put down the bowls to shake his hand.

"The Sasquatch Caves," I said. "We call them the Sasquatch Caves."

"Ah!" he laughed. "Remember those aspens with the big claw marks grown right into the bark? I wonder if they're still there."

"We'll hike out there," Lill said. "The girls can come."

We hadn't been out there since the RCMP had come to secure the area and take the pilot out.

"I *would* like to see the crash site," said Larry.

It was hard to dislike Larry, as much as I wanted to. I was sure he was bringing bad news. But at breakfast he told us stories about when the school was a lodge that his family ran. If a guest was mean to the kids, Larry and his younger brother, Luke, used to catch a frog or a toad and release it into the guest's bedroom. Then they got to play the hero when they were called to remove it. Their parents never guessed.

"They had all sorts of theories about how the frogs got into the rooms—in a boot, or on the firewood, or in the laundry."

Lill, Lucy and Larry, all three of them suddenly looked younger, their faces open with bright smiles.

"Have you been tobogganing yet this year?" Larry asked.

"Not yet," said Lucy. "We've been too busy."

"Let's go tobogganing," Lill said. "We'll make a fire and have a picnic."

"Egg salad sandwiches, hot chocolate and marshmallows," said Meredith, jumping up. "I'll boil the eggs for you."

"Well, I guess I can't say no," said Larry.

After breakfast, Lucy and Meredith were driving into town to spend the day at the hospital with Jasie. John-Lee was still there, too, but Diamond had been released the day after they arrived and she was at a hotel waiting until it was safe to move John-Lee.

"*I have a view of the lake,*" she wrote in an email. "*I'm writing songs! Jasie looks good. She's sleeping peacefully. When she wakes up, she'll find a room full of flowers—tiger lilies, for her fierce heart.*"

I tried to keep a picture of that in my mind.

We spent the day on the tobogganing hill by the creek. It was good to be outside, our leg muscles burning from the trudge up the hill pulling the toboggans and our cheeks warm from the fresh air.

Larry and Grace packed snow into a chute at the bottom of the hill so that the toboggans shot out onto a flat frozen part of the creek. We took turns shoveling snow to clear an area that we'd use for skating if it stayed cold.

Lill built a fire and as the setting sun shone a golden orange path down the creek, we settled next to it with hot chocolate steaming up into our faces. We sat quietly watching the flames. But in the quiet, my mind went back to the same place. I didn't know about Larry, but for the rest of us, I was pretty sure there was only one thing on our minds: Jasie.

Later, after dinner, I went to our room and discovered Danny already there, seated at the desk with her head bent over several pages covered in numbers and calculations.

"What are you doing?" I asked.

She whirled in her chair, her face bright.

"I have an idea!" she said.

I kicked off my shoes and climbed onto my bed. "Okay."

"I'm going to call a meeting tomorrow with everybody. Not the sisters, not yet."

"Can you tell me now?"

She held up a page of notes and numbers, neatly arranged in rows. "It's the Green Mountain Academy Outdoor Survival Weekend Workshops. If we could hold outdoor camps on the weekend for kids from town, we could earn probably a couple thousand a month for the school. We could teach them to set up a camp, build a fire, use a compass . . ." She stopped.

"You don't seem all that excited," she said.

"No, I am. It's a great idea. It's just hard to think of anything right now. All I can think about is that it's my fault Jasie is in a coma."

"No one said coma."

"Well, why won't she wake up?"

Danny put down her pencil and turned so that her eyes met mine.

"I'm going to tell you something my grandma told me." She took a deep breath. "You're not that important."

"What?"

"That didn't come out right. I mean, you're important, you're my best friend. But you're not so important that everything is because of what you did. Not everything is your fault. Your dad, Jasie. They made decisions too. Grandma would say you're as important as our bent pine tree. The rocks. The rain, the stars. That's pretty important. No less than them, but no more either. Does that make sense?"

It was starting to. I could feel something in my heart letting go, like a fist loosening.

"Each of us has a part. Each of us needs each other. It's not all on you."

Tears I didn't even know I'd been holding in spilled over and ran down my cheeks.

Danny sniffed back her own tears.

"It's not like I always remember it either," she said. "I needed the reminder myself."

"Your grandma sounds like my grandma," I said.

Then we both cried as the night outside our bedroom window grew darker.

Danny got up and went for glasses of water and brought back cool cloths for our tear-streaked faces.

"Do you think Larry might change his mind?" she asked. "He had such fun today, maybe he sees . . ."

"I was thinking that too. And with your idea to bring in extra money . . ."

"I can't wait to ask the other girls what they think."

When the moon rose beyond our window curtains like a luminous, fragile shell, it felt like a familiar friend watching over us.

CHAPTER TWENTY-NINE

We tried to pretend we weren't waiting.

Meredith and Carmen practiced a piano duet they'd been trying to learn. Grace went outside to chop kindling, her way of relieving stress, and amid the chords and melody of piano came the rhythmic chop of the ax and hollow clop of wood being tossed in a pile.

Ming and Lindsay played canasta at the dining room table, their murmurs rising and falling behind the fans of their cards. At the other end of the table, I played solitaire with a snap of each card I laid down. And at the middle of the table, Danny's pencil crayon scratched across her sketch pad. She'd drop a green pencil and pick up a brown one, drop the brown and pick up green. Snap, snap, plink, chop.

All of these sounds of waiting echoed and hung there in the great room like a fog that wouldn't clear as we waited for another sound: a door to open, footsteps on the stairs. Over an hour ago, Lucy, Lill and Larry had gone upstairs to the room that served as Lucy's office. We knew that this was the meeting that had been temporarily delayed while Lucy was in town at the hospital. It was the reason Larry had flown all the way from Toronto, rented a truck and driven out to the school. No one thought his visit was for fun and no one thought it didn't matter.

Danny had called all of us together for our own meeting after breakfast and she told everyone her idea for the weekend workshops. Everyone, even Grace, liked the idea. But no one thought it would be enough to save the school.

After a while the sounds melted into the background and one sound I'd never noticed before became the only thing I could hear—the *tick, tick, tick* of the clock on the great room wall. Danny crumpled up her paper and tore off a new one. I couldn't concentrate either.

Finally, there was a click from the door upstairs and a squawk of hinges. We all looked up from what we were doing and searched each other's eyes, as if we'd find answers there. Steps on the stairs. One person. Then the vacuum suck of the back door opening and a quiet thud as it was pulled closed.

Meredith and Carmen stopped playing. Ming and Lindsay laid down their cards. Danny's pencil hovered in mid-air.

Who had left and where were they going?

An engine roared to life in the yard.

"Who was that?" said Meredith, jumping to her feet to check at the same moment that Grace came bursting through the front door, still holding the ax.

"Where is he going?" she said. Her eyes swept the room wildly.

"Larry?" said Meredith.

"There is only one 'he' in this house," said Grace.

"That can't be good," Lindsay said quietly.

But my brain wanted to find a way to make it fit, to make it still okay, to find some reason that Larry sneaking out the back door without saying goodbye could be a good thing.

It was at least ten minutes before we heard more footsteps on the stairs. During that time, it seemed we'd barely breathed. My hands began to sweat as the sisters came down the hall.

Their faces said it all. I had never seen Lucy look so defeated. Her skin had lost its normal rosy glow and instead looked gray and drawn. Her eyes were downcast, her hands in her pockets. Lill went to the fireplace and turned her back to us, drawing a handful of kindling from the box and arranging it in the grate.

Lucy just stood in the doorway. Finally, as we stared at her, she took a deep breath.

"We have to talk," she said. "Let's sit down."

Everyone was sitting already except for Grace, Lucy and Lill, but we got up and followed her to the couch and chairs by the fireplace. Grace stood very still.

"I'm afraid I have some bad news," she began. "We've looked at every option, but . . ."

She swallowed, struggling to go on.

Lill said nothing, still half turned away.

"The school will have to close by Christmas."

Grace dropped the ax to the carpet.

"What's going to happen to me?" she said. "Everyone has somewhere to go except me."

She ran out of the room before she could hear the answer.

If I could have opened my mouth to speak, I probably would have said the same thing. But I couldn't speak. My whole body had tightened—my jaw, chest, lips, brain—like it was folding in on itself.

That night felt like one of the longest nights of my life. During dinner, none of us could look at each other. Even Meredith, who could usually be counted on to cheer us up or at least annoy everyone by trying, was quiet. Lill talked about driving to town to see Jasie the next day and she and Lucy worked out the seating arrangements for the SUV: Lucy and Meredith, who'd already seen her, would stay home to make room for the rest of us. In flat, quiet voices, they went through details they didn't need to, just so that, I thought, maybe we would not notice that there was absolutely nothing they could say to make this better.

CHAPTER THIRTY

Pine and cedar scented the air as we sat knee-to-knee in the SUV. The road had been plowed and sanded; sun brightened a blue-blue sky and lit up puffs of frothy white clouds. It was a perfect day.

A plane crossed the sky high above the trees and disappeared. On any other Sunday, we'd be in the woods exploring, gathering wood, walking the trails and making new ones. Today we'd only gone far enough to gather boughs and sprigs to make forest bouquets for Jasie.

On any other drive to town, which took between an hour and an hour and a half, depending on the road conditions, someone would play music on her phone and we'd all sing along. Meredith and Carmen had the best voices and assigned us various parts—high harmony, low harmony, melody. Sometimes we sang without the phone music.

Today we rode along in quiet. Lill concentrated on her driving. In spite of the sanding, there were some slippery sections. The road dipped and rose, rounded bends and straightened out again, snow-covered pines lining both sides. As we got closer to town, cell service blinked in briefly, some of the girls' phones beeped with their incoming messages, then it dropped out again. I wondered where Aunt Sissy had been when she'd gotten the call from the sheriff about Dad.

We came into town and drove right past my old school— and the playground where Carly and I used to hang upside down on the monkey bars waiting for her mom. I missed Carly a little, but she was part of my old life. I didn't want to try to go back to it. Whatever happened, I decided then, I would not move back to Penticton with Grandpa. I couldn't.

For Christmas I would be in Vancouver with Aunt Sissy. We'd go see Mom and she might be able to go for a walk around the hospital grounds. After that . . . I couldn't picture anything after that.

With our armloads of fragrant forest bouquets, we crowded into the hospital room where Jasie lay, tiny and peaceful-looking, as Diamond had said. Her long black hair was loose and coiled over one shoulder. The tiger lilies Diamond had brought matched the sunny yellow room. Jasie's parents were on their way home from Africa, but they would be at least another day or two.

Meredith took the chair by Jasie's head. She'd brought her hairbrush and elastics and she began gently brushing Jasie's thick glossy hair.

At first no one knew what to say. Then Danny said, "Lilac misses you. She goes into your room and comes out meowing."

Then Lindsay told her about our tobogganing afternoon and soon the room was full of noise and laughter. Meredith braided Jasie's hair into a neat single side braid and pinned a sprig of kinnikinnick into it behind her ear. Everyone took turns taking photos with her.

She seemed completely fine except for the fact that she hadn't opened her eyes. Lill left to speak to the nurses and we arranged the kinnikinnick and pine boughs and sprigs of Oregon grape in mason jars tied with red ribbons and placed them around the room. We would meet Diamond and John-Lee afterward. John-Lee was due to leave the hospital in a couple of days.

Each of us took turns squeezing Jasie's hand as we said goodbye. Some of the girls had already filed out of the room. When it was Danny's turn, she gave a little shriek.

"She squeezed it back!" she said.

"Are you sure?"

"I'm positive."

"You could have imagined it."

"I didn't. She absolutely positively squeezed my hand."

Danny's face shone with excitement. The other girls piled back in, everyone talking at once.

"Let's not overwhelm her," Lill said, shushing us. But I could see she was excited, too.

"She hears us, I know she does," Danny said. "I don't want to leave her alone. Can I stay here? I could sleep on the floor, I don't mind."

"I don't think they'll allow that," Lill said.

❖

"Stay with me," said Diamond when she heard the news. "I've got an extra bed in my hotel room and we can come back to see her first thing. You can spend as long in Jasie's room tomorrow as they'll let you."

It was decided that Danny and I would be the ones to stay.

"It's only fair," said Ming. "You two are the closest to Jasie."

❖

Diamond's guitar sat propped against the chair next to the window. The case lay on the bed. It had survived the crash, miraculously without any damage. The red suitcase I'd dug through to find the running shoe was also barely damaged, and now sat open on the luggage rack. There was nothing in this room to hint that someone in it had survived a plane crash.

"Come in," Diamond said. She went to the desk and tidied some papers, tucking them into a folder. "This is another new song," she said. "But it's a big secret." She winked.

That night we ordered pizza and ate it looking out at the lights sparkling on Okanagan Lake. Though it was cold, we sat on the balcony afterward with the hotel blankets over our shoulders and we waited for the moon to rise over the mountains.

"These little things mean a lot more to me now," Diamond said. "Too bad I had to fall out of a plane to learn that. You girls have a special life out there at that school."

Danny and I looked at each other. Then we told her what had happened, that it had finally been decided that the school would close before Christmas. Diamond frowned and fell quiet.

After the moon rose, we went back inside and watched a "mindless" movie, as Diamond called it.

The next day, Jasie opened her eyes.

CHAPTER THIRTY-ONE

"This one," said Grace. She grabbed the spruce tree by the middle of its trunk and shook the snow from it.

"It's a good shape," Lindsay agreed.

"It's big," said Ming.

"There's lots of room. This is the one," Grace said.

"Okay. Let's do it."

Grace swung her pack to the ground and pulled out the saw.

"I'm making a fire," Meredith said. "That's what we do every year."

"This isn't every year," Grace said. "I don't know why we're even getting this stupid tree."

"Lucy wanted it. They still have to be here over Christmas to get the place ready to sell. I can't even imagine."

"It's depressing," said Ming. Everyone looked at her. Meredith was the cheerful one, but Ming was our rock— even-tempered, practical and almost always in a good mood.

"A fire can't hurt," Meredith said. "Everything's better with a fire."

"Can you just stop?" Grace shouted, leveling a look at Meredith. "Can you just stop trying to pretend that everything will be fine? You're so relentlessly sunny ALL THE TIME. This is crappy. Can we just be allowed to feel crappy?"

Meredith sniffed and turned away.

"Whoever wants to help me . . . ," she said and set off into the trees to find wood.

Danny and I followed her.

"They're both right," Danny said.

Meredith didn't yet know where she'd be going after Christmas. She'd shuffle between her parents' places for the holidays, she said. They couldn't stand to be in the same room together. Her father did something to do with banking and spent most of his time out of the country, in Dubai or London or Hong Kong. Her mother lived in a penthouse apartment in Vancouver. When Meredith had called her from town about the school closing, she'd shouted at Meredith so loudly and for so long, we'd all heard it. Meredith had held her phone away from her ear and rolled her eyes. We heard her mother shout, "This is so inconvenient."

"Maybe I'll go to your school if I can get in," Meredith had said to Ming.

"Don't do it," Ming had answered.

So Grace was right. There was no way to pretend that everything was fine. But Meredith was right too. Everything *was* better with a fire.

As we sat around it later, Meredith spoke. "I get it that you're upset. We all are. But imagine what it must be like for the sisters. They've lived here since they were kids. The school will probably be torn down. There'll be a big hotel and a bunch of condos. So many of these beautiful old trees will be cleared." Her face clouded in tears she tried to hold back. "The least we can do is try to make it a little easier for them."

❖

After the fire, we dragged the tree back and set it up, filling the great room with the fresh fragrance of spruce and sap. An accountant had driven out to the school and was in an all-day meeting with the sisters that was still going on. Lill stepped out of the office to make coffee.

"Trade you places?" she said, stopping to admire the tree.

Meredith made shortbread cookies and laid the cookie sheets out on the table so we could decorate them.

"I'm good at a lot of things, but not this," Grace said suddenly.

Everyone looked up from what they were doing. It was rare for Grace to admit she might not be good at something.

"What are you doing?" Carmen asked.

"Writing a letter. Well, an email." Her legs were slung over a chair in front of the fireplace and she had the end of the pen in her teeth.

"I'm pretty good at writing," said Carmen. "Do you want me to help you?" She was being modest. Carmen wrote songs so good they made me cry.

I watched, wondering what Grace would say. I had never seen her ask for help with anything.

"I've started it," Grace said. "But I don't know what to say next."

"What have you got so far?"

Grace picked up her notebook and read, "*Dear Soleil. How are you? I am fine.*"

"You're writing to Soleil?" said Carmen.

"What makes you think that?" Grace answered in her driest voice.

Carmen laughed. "Okay," she said. "Forget about what you think people are supposed to write in letters. Like 'How are you?' Do you even care?"

Grace thought about that. "Sort of. Not really. No."

"Exactly. So, scratch that out."

"But that's half my letter so far."

"Doesn't matter. If you start at the wrong place, you'll go in the wrong direction. Or nowhere at all."

"Okay, so what, then?" Grace said impatiently.

"Well, what do you really want to say?"

"I want to say I'm sorry I made her feel bad, but it was nothing personal."

"Hmm. Can I give you some advice?"

"I'm asking for advice."

"If you're going to say you're sorry, just stop there. Don't make excuses about it."

"Huh. Good point."

She sat with her pen poised above the page. She wrote a word, then tore the page from her notebook and crumpled it up.

"What?" said Carmen.

"This is hard. Like I can't just start a letter saying I'm sorry."

"How about you tell her about what we're doing right now? Tell her about the tree, how we picked it out, and had a fire, and now we're going to decorate cookies."

"That sounds dumb," she said. Then a minute later, "Okay. I'll try it."

After a few minutes bent over her notebook and scribbling, Grace sat up straighter. "It's pretty good. It's way better. I hope she doesn't think I'm just saying sorry because I'm trying to save the school."

"Well, are you?"

"Partly. But it's not just that. I realize that I've been wanting to keep the school to myself. But it doesn't work that way. It needs to be shared. I was stupid not to see that."

"Write that," Carmen said.

"Really?"

"You asked for my advice. That's my advice."

Lill and Lucy, looking flushed and tired, finally came out of the office with the accountant, a white-haired man wearing a sweater, down vest and scarf.

"Stay for dinner," Lucy said to him.

"No, thank you. It's tempting, but I don't want to tackle that road in the dark. It was bad enough in daylight," he said. "Girls, I heard a little of your story. I just want to say that each and every one of you is an inspiration."

He shook each of our hands, then he bundled up even more in his parka, hat and boots and he was gone.

"I thought we weren't supposed to talk to anyone about what happened," Grace said as soon as he was out the door.

Lucy had bent over the cookies and was decorating a large Santa with red and white sparkles. She seemed reluctant to answer Grace.

Lill, too, had turned away to hang a delicate glass star from one of the spruce limbs.

After a minute, she said, "He's Diamond and John-Lee's uncle. How about some music? Let's try to lighten up a little."

Dinner was quiet at first, so quiet the sound of forks and knives clinking on plates grew louder and louder. Then both Lill and Lucy went to speak at the same moment.

"Listen—"

"By the way—"

"You go."

"No, you go ahead."

Lucy cleared her throat. "I just wanted to let you know we're having some visitors tomorrow."

"Who?" everyone asked.

"It's a secret," said Lill. "A surprise."

"It has to be Jasie," Danny said.

We had not seen Jasie since she'd been released from the hospital. Her parents had arrived from Burkina Faso and they'd all flown straight to Calgary, where Jasie's grandparents lived. But we'd heard that she would make a full recovery.

"It won't be a surprise if we tell you," Lill said. "Let's just make the place look nice and festive."

"Fake it, you mean," said Grace.

"If that's what it takes, yes."

CHAPTER THIRTY-TWO

A white SUV drove into the yard the next day, followed by a black pickup truck.

Two people we didn't know got out of the truck and went to the back of it, where they opened the box and began pulling out tripods and black boxes.

Lill opened the front door wide. "Do you need a hand?" she called.

Then we saw Diamond, getting out of the SUV. She was helping John-Lee, whose arm was in a cast and who was trying to walk using one crutch. He gave us a big smile.

The back passenger seat opened and there was Jasie. She jumped down and ran to us. A ruckus of hugs and squeals and shouts filled the room.

But after hugging each of us, Diamond was all business.

She scanned the great room. "There's your piano," she said. "Perfect." She went over to it and took out the folder we'd seen on the desk in her hotel room.

The two people from the truck introduced themselves.

"I'm Laisha and that's Pip," one said. "We're from CBC Radio."

They busied themselves setting up recording equipment and cameras while we met Jasie's parents, Manraj and Anita, who had driven the SUV.

"What's going on?" Meredith asked.

"Wait and see," John-Lee said.

When everyone was finally settled, Diamond turned on the piano seat and spoke to the camera.

"By now, most of you know that my brother and I were in a plane crash. Our friend and pilot, Rico, didn't survive. But the story of how we survived hasn't yet been told. Today is the right time to tell it."

The camera followed her eyes as she told the story. Her descriptions were so vivid it was as if we were back out there, creeping on knees through the cave with Jasie. We were there as the girls loaded John-Lee into the sled. She told about Green Mountain Academy and its goals.

And she told about the song she'd written. "You helped us, now we're helping you," she said. "We want girls to hear about the school. All the proceeds from the song will go to Green Mountain Academy. If you're a girl who feels more at home in a forest than a regular classroom, maybe you'll come and join these brave girls."

Jasie's parents spoke next. "We're so proud of our courageous daughter," they began.

They explained Jasie's role in the rescue and then said they'd be making a scholarship in her name to help a girl who wanted to come to the school but couldn't afford the fees.

"The song is called 'When I Fall,'" Diamond said. "It's dedicated to the girls of Green Mountain Academy."

Her fingers struck the piano keys and she and John-Lee sang it together, taking turns on the verses. On the chorus, they sang together in perfect harmony.

No one wants to appear small.
We fake it every day.
I march to my drum, you to yours.
Is there any other way?

The mountains rise,
wind blows us astray,
and the course we try to stay.

But when I fall you help me up.
In the cold and snow,
you'll be there I know,
and when I fall you help me up.
Like the strongest pine,
hand in hand we climb.

As the song ended, Danny turned to Jasie, who was sitting between us. "Does this mean you're staying?"

"Yes, it does," Jasie said. "And I never thought I'd be saying this, but I wouldn't want to be anywhere else."

She took each of our hands in hers and held on.

CHAPTER THIRTY-THREE

I didn't go to the city for Christmas. Meredith, Grace and of course the sisters stayed too. On Christmas Eve, we took thermoses of spiced apple cider and the makings of s'mores and went out to the creek to clean the ice for skating. It had snowed earlier in the day, but the sky had cleared and the air seemed to shimmer in the starlight as Grace readied the wood for our fire.

I skimmed my shovel across the ice, passing Meredith as she cleared from the other side. Lucy and Lill set up the lawn chairs that they'd stored nearby under a tarp. Each of us worked quietly, lost in our own thoughts.

My thoughts were with Mom. Aunt Sissy said she might be able to bring her to her apartment, if Mom was having one of her "good days." I had never spent a Christmas without Mom. But it wasn't my own loneliness I was worried about. I had the sisters, and Grace and Meredith, and the peaceful beauty of the forest in winter to keep me company. Mom had only memories and the shadows that haunted her mind.

Skating brought some noise to the night—the clean slice of blades on ice, then our laughter as we tried pirouettes and figure eights and Lucy and Lill raced each other end to end on our small rink.

Later, we sat by the fire and roasted marshmallows for our s'mores.

"We've got so many new applications," said Lucy. "Our problem now is how to pick students. We can only take seven or eight more."

"But save one spot," Grace said.

"Save one?"

"For Soleil. I sent her an email."

Lucy and Lill were quiet for a minute, then Lill said, "I'm sure she appreciates that, Grace, but I think Soleil made her decision."

Back at the school, we stayed up late playing Yahtzee on the floor in front of the fireplace.

At a break in the game, I noticed Grace slip away and quietly pad down the hall of the old wing. Her bedroom wasn't down there, so I wondered what she was doing.

When she came back to the game, she was smiling.

"What are you smiling about?" Meredith said.

"Can't I smile?"

"You can smile. It's just that you usually . . ."

She plopped down on the rug. "Sorry, Lucy, I went in your upstairs room," she said.

"You don't look very sorry," Lucy said.

"I'm not." Her smile widened to a grin that I had never seen on Grace's face. "I checked my email. Soleil answered. She wants to come back."

❖

We didn't finish our game of Yahtzee. Lill made a little speech and we celebrated with glasses of apple cider and pretzels. Everyone was too excited to sleep, but when I couldn't keep my eyes open any longer, I went down the hall of the old wing to Danny's and my bedroom, still hearing the soft voices of Lill and Lucy by the fire, working out room assignments for the new students.

The room felt empty without Danny. Tired as I was, I didn't sleep for a long time, but lay watching the patterns of moon shadows moving across the wall.

It was eleven before I woke up the next morning. I had never slept so late on a Christmas morning. But I didn't jump out of bed. The smell of coffee and baking told me the others were up. Meredith had said she'd make cinnamon buns this morning. But still I lay there. I would not think of Christmas, I decided. Instead, I remembered that Lucy had promised we'd skate on the creek again today. I focused on that—the push off and the slice of skate blades gliding on ice in the clean, cold air, the surrounding pine trees weighed down with snow.

I heard a car coming up the hill to the school. As far as I knew, we weren't expecting guests, and I wasn't in the mood to talk to strangers. Maybe I could stay in bed a little longer, hope it was just someone looking for directions.

But I heard car doors opening, then shouts of surprise.

I would have to get up and be polite.

I dressed and gathered my hair in a semi-tidy ponytail. Fresh air wafted down the hall as I headed to the great room. But it was not strangers who stood stomping their feet on the mat.

It was Aunt Sissy and Mom. The smile Mom gave me was a Christmas present I hadn't imagined.

That afternoon I would show Mom the trail to the creek, the bent pine, the tracks that rabbits had made in the snow, and the place below our skating rink where water gurgled out and continued snaking under a speckled shell of ice to the valley below.

Mom would lace on a pair of school skates, and when she wobbled onto the ice, I would see her laugh for the first time in a long time.

The End

ACKNOWLEDGEMENTS

The story for Green Mountain Academy came to me from two sources. Many years ago, on my first date with David, whom I would later marry, we hiked into the mountains and came across the wreckage of a plane crash. It was recent. No one was at the scene, but otherwise, it looked very much like what I described in the novel: luggage, some of it unopened, was strewn on the ground. The images have never left me. Some time later, I dreamt of a plane crash near the grounds of a girls' school. I don't know how I knew it was a girls' school, but when I woke from the dream, I "remembered" that detail. My friend Anne McDonald, who is also a writer, asked me when I would be turning that dream into a novel. Thanks for the encouragement, Anne! I finally found the place to tell it.

The idea for the Sasquatch Caves stems from stories David shared with me about caves he played in as a child when his family lived near Hope, BC. David is a member of the Stó:lō Nation in British Columbia, a region where Sasquatch lives. Many First Nations in British Columbia have traditional stories about

Sasquatch, who goes by many different names. My portrayal in the book doesn't attempt to tell those traditional stories.

Ideas for campfire songs were provided by Anna Draper. I'm also grateful to Anna's family, Sophia, Jay and Barb Johnston, for their unwavering dedication to my writing life.

The Saskatchewan Writers' Guild's retreat at St. Peter's Abbey has been a mainstay of my writing career, providing invaluable opportunities for me to get work done in a quiet, supportive environment. I thank the Guild and the monks of St. Peter's profoundly. I'd also like to thank the Banff Centre Leighton Artist Studios, Dorland Mountain Arts Colony, the Naramata Centre and BC Arts Council for the writing time and space their programs offered.

I'd like to acknowledge the inspiring contributions of my father-in-law, Dan Joyce, to my knowledge of all things outdoors. If I have a question about the British Columbia wilderness, he can be counted on for the answer. Surandar Dasanjh and Marcy Trotter at Okanagan College also patiently answered my many questions. Likewise, I appreciate the thoughtful feedback from Frances Bolton and Terrena Buck.

Denise Bukowski, my agent, is always on my side, and I thank her deeply for years of guidance and support. Thank you to my editor at Penguin, Lynne Missen, for her sensitivity and patient suggestions that helped to shape this story. And thanks to Linda Pruessen for careful copy editing.

My family, Anne, Mary, Pat, Barbie and Neil, continue to ground me with their love and wisdom. I'm grateful to have them to turn to when I have doubts about my direction, both in life and in writing.

Thank you, Khal Joyce, for your love, for being an avid reader, and for enthusiastically sharing my books with other readers. To David Joyce, my partner in this writing adventure and all my adventures: I have endless gratitude for your love and stories that inspire and nourish my work.